More Than Love

by

Sharon C. Cooper

Disclaimer
This story is a work of fiction. Names, characters, and
incidents are either products of the author's imagination or
are used fictitiously. Any resemblance to actual events,
locales, organizations or persons, living or dead, is entirely
coincidental.

Chapter One

"Want something else to eat, son?"

Benjamin Jenkins glanced at his mother, Katherine, as he ate the last forkful of smothered chicken and rice on his plate. "I'm good, Mom, but thanks. As usual, dinner was excellent."

"Dang, Momma. You didn't ask if I had enough to eat," his sister, Carolyn Jenkins-Richwood, grumbled with mock disgust.

Ben stopped by his parents' estate after work at least once during the week to check on them, and again on Sunday for the family's weekly brunch. With six brothers and sisters, a ton of nieces and nephews, and a few great-nieces and nephews, it was rare to show up and not have other family members present.

Today, it was Carolyn. She was sitting across from him rolling her eyes.

Standing, she walked across the huge kitchen to the center island and grabbed another slice of bread. "I always knew big-headed Ben was your favorite."

Ben grinned, not surprised by her comment. Even in their fifties, his siblings still took every opportunity to complain that he was the favorite child.

He shrugged. "What can I say? It's true."

"Now y'all know I don't have favorites. I love all of you

1

the same," their mother said as she wiped down the kitchen counter. That was her standard line whenever the conversation came up. It might've been true that she loved them all the same. Katherine Jenkins had a way of making everyone feel special.

After rinsing his plate and placing it in the dishwasher, Ben draped his arm around his mother's shoulders and kissed her on the cheek. There weren't enough words in his vocabulary to describe how much he loved the woman. She was the heartbeat of the Jenkins family, and he couldn't imagine a life without her in it.

Growing up, his parents were always present. His father used to put in a lot of hours getting Jenkins & Sons Construction on the map, while his mother took care of them and the household. Yet, one of them always showed up at their kid's school events, sporting activities, and was always there to get them out of jams. They made raising the seven of them look easy.

With two boys of his own, Ben knew better. Raising children—and now parenting adult kids—was no easy feat, which made him respect his parents all the more. There was nothing he wouldn't do for either of them.

His heart fluttered as he smiled down at his mother. In her late seventies, with her long salt-and-pepper hair pulled into a ponytail at the nape of her neck, she still looked youthful. She had a few laugh lines at the corners of her eyes and mouth, but she could easily pass for someone twenty years her junior.

Considerably shorter than his six feet, his prissy mother had ruled her household like a master sergeant in the military and put the fear of God in all of them. Most of the time without raising her voice.

No one would dare cross her or talk back. They knew better.

"There's so much food left. Take some for lunch tomorrow," she said, lovingly patting his cheek before moving out of his hold. She grabbed a carryout container from the pantry and started filling it.

"What about everyone else?" Ben poured himself a glass of lemonade. "I'm sure there will be others stopping by this evening."

"There's plenty," his mother insisted. She lived to take care of her family. Cooking for them was just one of many ways she expressed her love.

Ben's cell phone buzzed, and he pulled it from his pants pocket. A slow smile kicked up the corners of his mouth and warmth spread through his body when he glanced at the screen.

Makena.

The woman who starred in his nightly fantasies. The woman he could see spending the rest of his life with. And the woman who insisted they just be friends.

Makena Nichols. His best friend.

Ben skimmed the text.

MN: Are we still on for tonight?

He loved this woman and would do anything for her, but spending a Friday night painting a home office didn't sound like fun. Especially since his youngest son, Ben Junior—or as the family referred to him, BJ—was a painter by trade. All it would take was a phone call to get the room taken care of in a couple of hours.

Ben typed a quick reply.

BEN: Change of plans. Friday night painting—not interested. You and me—jazz club.

MK: Ben, you promised.

Ben smiled. He could picture her gorgeous, pouty lips turning into a frown as she glared at the phone.

BEN: I promised we'd get your room painted. I'll get BJ to paint.

Seconds ticked by without her responding. Unlike most people Ben knew, especially in the legal field, Makena's way of relaxing was doing projects around the house. That was okay sometimes, but he was on a mission. He was determined to prove to her that they were more than friends.

After her divorce, Makena had moved back to Cincinnati almost two years ago with her daughter, Ava. Now that Ava was in college, Makena was ready to date. Except, according to her, dating Ben wasn't an option. Never mind that he was crazy in love with her and wanted to take their relationship beyond the friend zone.

MK: Send BJ over to help paint, and you go to the club.

Ben laughed out loud, then ducked his head when he realized his sister was watching him. He typed his response.

BEN: You're not funny. I'll be there.

He didn't have to wait long for her response.

MK: K. And bring dessert.

Grinning, Ben shook his head and shoved his phone back into his pocket. He ignored his sister's knowing look as he thought about Makena. He had to convince her that their friendship wouldn't be in jeopardy if they dated. They'd known each other for over forty years, growing up in the same neighborhood. That day in third grade, when he fought off a kid bullying her, was the day they became friends.

The older they got, the closer they grew. Yet, they never crossed that friendship line. After going their separate ways, to different colleges, then law school, they tried to keep in touch. But their lives moved in various directions.

Makena had lived in Columbus and married a junior partner at the law firm where she worked shortly after law school. A year later, Ben married, but he soon realized he married the wrong woman. But he had grown up believing that divorce wasn't an option. When you married, you stayed married, and he had every intention of making the relationship work.

Yet, the constant arguing and being accused of one thing after another—including cheating—started to wear on him. He questioned his own sanity, wondering what he'd been thinking marrying a woman who didn't trust him.

There had even been times when he wondered if he had gotten married because Makena had married.

Ben would never know. All he knew was that divorcing his wife and putting his two boys through the resulting emotional turmoil had been one of the hardest things he'd ever experienced.

"Do you have a date for the community center fundraiser on Saturday?" Carolyn asked, cutting into Ben's thoughts. "Before you say no, let me inform you that Sydney Greer will be there. I saw her the other day. If you go without a plus-one, she'll be all over you."

Just hearing the insufferable woman's name sent anxiety spiking through Ben's veins. Sydney was the last person he wanted to run into. She'd been trying to hook up with him for years, in between her numerous marriages.

"If you don't have a date, I know the perfect person you—"

"No," Ben said before Carolyn could finish.

The women in his family, his sisters as well as his nieces, were always trying to fix him up with someone.

"I can find my own date."

His law firm had purchased a table for the event, and he was expected to attend. And there was only one woman in the world he would ever consider going with.

"Let me guess. You're going to ask Mac," his sister said, referring to Makena by her childhood nickname.

"I can't think of a better person to take as my plus-one." He and Makena spent what little free time they had together. Dinners. Movie nights. They even carved out time during the weekend to hang out.

They were also always each other's date for events. Technically, he was dating her without the official label. Well, that and Makena didn't think he was serious about pursuing her. Now that she was seriously thinking about dating other men, Ben really needed to up his game.

He had to show her that she was his; that they belong together and have for nearly four decades...ever since third grade.

But how? How could he convince her that they belonged

together?

Carolyn shook her head. "I don't know why you guys keep pretending you're only friends. We all know the real deal."

"Leave him alone," their mother said, placing a shopping bag with the food she had packed in front of him. "If she's *the one* it'll happen in time."

There was a Jenkins family myth that had been around for generations, claiming that when a Jenkins man meets *the one*, he immediately knows. Makena had always held a special spot in his heart. Ben just hadn't realized how much she meant to him until she married another man.

Now that he and Makena were back in each other's lives, Ben was ready to take their relationship to the next level. Yet, each time he brought up the subject, she'd say something about not wanting to ruin their friendship. He wasn't giving up, though.

Soon. She'll be mine soon.

*

Makena sat at her round conference table and couldn't stop staring at her new client. Edward Foxall was the splitting image of what Ben would probably look like in thirty years. The resemblance was spooky. Not only did they have the same cinnamon skin tone, facial features, and similar build, but they also had some of the same facial expressions. But what really held her captive was his eyes. He had the same light-brown eyes as her Ben.

They have to be related, she thought. But Makena knew most of Ben's family, and had never seen this guy before. The resemblance was probably just a coincidence.

"I'm debt-free, and I've already given away almost everything of value," Edward explained. He removed the small portable oxygen tank from the conference table and set it in the chair next to him. After adjusting the oxygen tubes hanging from his nose, he continued. "Drawing up my will won't take long."

When he first walked into the office with his caregiver's assistance, Makena had wondered if he was mentally capable of making a will. They'd been chatting for the last fifteen minutes, and he was easy to talk to and had insisted she call him Edward. Makena soon learned that he was a prime example of why not to judge someone by the way they looked. He might've had physical limitations and needed the extra oxygen, but there was nothing wrong with his mind.

During the conversation, Makena learned that he served in the army for twenty-five years. After retiring from the military, he became a certified accountant, which he did for twenty years until retiring for good five years ago. Not only was Edward easy to talk to, he was also charming and a little flirtatious. His quick wit had her laughing through much of their discussion.

Makena typed information into the form on her laptop. "Okay, who are your beneficiaries, and what are you leaving them?"

"I only have one beneficiary, and I'm leaving him my land. Here's his contact information." Edward reached into the interior pocket of his black wool coat and pulled out a slip of paper. "His name is Benjamin Jenkins."

*

"Makena? Makena!"

Makena startled when her partner at the law firm, Halle Pierce, clapped her hands.

"That is the second time today that you've zoned out on me. What's up with you?"

Makena shook her head. "I'm sorry. I can't stop thinking about Edward Foxall. I'm still debating with myself on whether to tell Ben about him."

"I know how you feel about Ben, but you can't tell him. It'll be unethical."

Makena stared at her friend, wishing she could disagree.

For over a week, Makena had wanted to tell Ben about her new client. But as an attorney, she was bound by attorney-client privilege. It didn't matter that she trusted Ben more than anyone else in the world, except for maybe her daughter. Still, she had to keep her mouth shut.

Her throat tightened. The suffocating feeling had Makena gripping the edge of her desk. "Edward said that he and Ben never met, but what if they really are somehow related? Ben will never forgive me for not telling him."

It didn't help that her client looked as if he was living his last days. Even with the oxygen tank and his caretaker by his side, Edward was barely able to move around. Yet, his mind was sharp, and he was adamant about how he wanted his will drawn up.

Halle sighed and stood. She tugged on the tail of her short navy-blue suit jacket and smoothed out the matching pencil skirt. Beautiful inside and out, Halle always looked like she meant business whenever she stepped out of the house. She and Makena had similar taste in clothing. Their similarities, though, stopped there.

Halle, with her fair complexion and freckles sprinkled across her nose, had curly red hair that hung past her shoulders. She was five-ten, thin, and outspoken.

Makena was golden-brown with shoulder-length hair that she usually kept in a conservative bun. At five-six with womanly curves, she was more reserved than her friend.

"Ben could never be mad at you for long. He loves you. Heck, the man more than loves you. He worships the ground you walk on. In his eyes, you can do no wrong." Halle lifted a finger when Makena started to deny that claim. "Don't. Don't insult my intelligence and try to argue what we both know."

"Halle, listen."

"No. *You* listen. Just because you're keeping your head in the sand about your feelings for him doesn't mean they don't exist."

Of course she was right. Makena could admit to herself that she was *in* love with Ben, even if she was trying to fight her feelings. But changing their relationship status would just be too weird. They had too much history. How could they cross over from friend and confidant to sex-charged lovers? So what if he knew her better than anyone and was always only a phone call away… Makena couldn't cross that line.

Been there. Done that. Ended up divorced.

No. Ben meant everything to her. Stepping over that line was too much of a gamble.

She and her ex-husband Preston had started as good

friends. Yet, they couldn't make their relationship work. What if she and Ben became lovers and things didn't work out? Then Makena would lose him. The one man she could always count on. There would be no recovering from that type of loss.

"As for Ben," Halle continued, "he, more than anyone, will understand why you couldn't discuss your client with him."

"Yeah, maybe," Makena conceded, but a sinking feeling settled in her gut. If she lost Ben because of not sharing her suspicions about her client, she'd be devastated.

Chapter Two

An hour later, Makena headed home. As she drove through the streets of Cincinnati, she reflected on how much her life had changed in the last couple of years.

Shortly before she moved back to town, her parents had retired to Florida, selling their house to her. It was a win-win for all of them. The purchase gave her a place for her and Ava to live, while providing her parents the freedom and the money to finally start their retirement.

Makena was also working at a law firm that she was proud to be a part of and loved the people she worked with. For the first time in her career, she wasn't putting in twelve- to fifteen-hour days. Granted, she still put in the occasional long day, but it wasn't the norm anymore.

Then there was Ben. Having him in her life on a daily basis was like inhaling a breath of fresh air. He was such an important part of her world. Though they talked on occasion when she lived in Columbus, now they spent much of their free time together.

Makena turned onto her street and the corners of her mouth lifted into a smile at the sight of Ben's white Range Rover pulling into her driveway. They couldn't have timed their arrival better even if they had planned it.

As she pulled into the driveway, Makena pushed the

button for the garage door opener and watched as it slowly slid up. Ben drove into the garage and parked on the right-hand side, and she slid in on the left.

She had barely shut off her car and closed the overhead garage door when Ben appeared on the driver's side of her vehicle. Her heart did a little jig at the sight of him. It never failed, especially lately. Whenever she saw him or was in his presence, her body sparked to life and a tingling sensation skittered across her skin.

What was wrong with her? This was Ben. She shouldn't be having these feelings about her *friend*. It was getting harder and harder to deny that she wanted him as much as he claimed to want her.

Just stay strong, Makena reminded herself. *We have too much to lose.*

"Hey, beautiful," he said when he pulled the car door open. That suggestive grin—the one that always made her pulse beat a little faster—spread across his sexy lips.

"Hey, yourself." She shamelessly loved when he called her *beautiful, sweetheart,* or *baby.* The words seeped into her soul and always made her feel special and cherished. Was she that hard up for a romantic love that sweet terms of endearments made her giddy inside?

Yes came the loud voice in her head. She hadn't been intimate with a man since her ex-husband. Her mind and body craved the attention of a man, especially when that man was Ben.

Stop! Stop! Stop! She berated herself. This line of thinking had to stop before she did something stupid.

Like leap into his arms and tell him that she wanted him more than she wanted her next breath.

Makena grabbed hold of his gloved hand and let him pull her from the seat. "Thank you. I'm surprised you beat me here. How was your day?" she asked, grabbing her laptop case from the backseat.

"Better now. How was yours?"

She let them into the house and glanced at the shopping

bag and duffel bag in Ben's hands. It looked like he picked up more than dessert.

Makena went through her usual routine. She kicked off her shoes in the foyer, set her large handbag on the first step that led to the second floor, and went about turning on a couple of lights.

"So you were going to bail out and leave me with the painting, huh?" she asked, returning to the foyer.

Ben hung his overcoat in the front closet, not responding to her comment.

Makena jammed her hands on her hips. "Well?"

"I told you my plan for the painting. It would get done. Just not by us. I would've preferred to spend the evening with you listening to some live jazz."

He grinned and his dimples winked at her, sending a crackle of heat racing through her body. She should be immune to his boyish good looks, but lately, everything about the man turned her on.

God help me. I have to be strong.

Ben's appreciative gaze raked over her charcoal-gray skirted suit on down to the matching three-inch heels that buckled around the ankle. "You look gorgeous."

"Thank you." Makena always felt extra-feminine in the outfit.

As Ben continued taking her in, she did the same to him.

As a corporate lawyer, he wore a suit every day and not just any suit. Like the one he had on, they all molded perfectly to his fit body, as if tailored specifically for him. The brown tweed three-piece ensemble, paired with a beige shirt and print tie, looked like money. Sophisticated and powerful, similar to his personality. He was one of the nicest men she knew, but a force to be reckoned with in the courtroom.

Her gaze settled back on his face and the smoothness of his cinnamon-toned skin and his sensual mouth. Normally, she was attracted to rugged men, but Ben stimulated something so carnal inside of her. Something she had never experienced before, not even with Preston. Ben was always well groomed, clean-shaven, and meticulously dressed, but it was those pretty, light-brown eyes that made her heart do cartwheels inside her chest.

Makena swallowed hard. Those gorgeous eyes were still her weakness. She'd been attracted to Ben since they were kids. Back then, it had been a childhood crush, but that crush had blossomed into something so much stronger. Especially in the last six months. Something had shifted between them. Something powerfully intense.

The way he studied her and the slight smile on his sexy lips, made her cheeks heat. If Makena didn't know better, she would think he could read minds. Even if she insisted they just be friends, the way he was still checking her out should've been inappropriate. But she'd be lying if she said that she didn't like the attention.

"When are you going to stop running from me? Running from—"

"What's in the shopping bag?" she interrupted. He found every opportunity to bring up the subject. Unfortunately, it was getting harder and harder to shoot down the idea. The nightly dreams and daytime fantasies she'd been having of him weren't helping matters.

Ben stared at her, looking as if he wanted to say more. Instead, he headed to her kitchen and started pulling several food containers from the shopping bag.

"You cooked?"

He was an amazing cook and prepared meals for her whenever his busy schedule allowed.

"Not this time. Leftovers from my mom. You'll be happy to know she made a banana pudding." He held up a plastic see-through container. "Of course there's enough for two."

Makena grinned as she rinsed her hands in the kitchen sink. "Of course. She takes such good care of us." Makena had fond memories of her and her brothers hanging out at the Jenkins' house when they were kids. Theirs was the fun house and every visit included some type of food.

For the next few minutes, she and Ben sat at the small kitchen table talking while she munched on dinner. They agreed to save the banana pudding for after they painted. As they discussed their workday, she couldn't help but think how perfect it was to spend another Friday night with him.

After Makena finished eating, she and Ben changed into painting clothes. Now they stood in the middle of her home office where she had already covered the equipment and furniture. Looking around, Makena was starting to have second thoughts about the painting job. When she originally came up with the bright idea to do the painting herself, she forgot how much work was involved.

"Are you sure about this?" Ben asked dryly. "BJ is only a phone call away," he said of his youngest son the painter.

Makena looked around. They were going to have to prime one of the walls—the one that was currently burgundy—before they could paint it. The others that were beige should be fine to go over with the soft gray paint she had purchased.

"I'm sure. Let's do this."

Ben had already brought in the aluminum ladder from the garage. He started taping off the ceiling, while Makena started taping the baseboards.

She glanced at him when he climbed down the ladder, moved it over and went back up. It was no surprise that he was comfortable that high off the floor. When he and his siblings were growing up, they helped with the family's construction business.

Makena had been surprised that when his father, Steven Jenkins, was ready to retire, no one wanted to take over the business. At least not until Ben's niece, Peyton, stepped forward. Her leadership turned the company into a multimillion-dollar business that had been thriving ever since.

They worked in silence, making quick work of protecting the ceiling and baseboards until Ben asked, "Do you know the proper way to paint?" He explained the importance of starting with cutting in, where the paintbrush is used first to take care of the areas too hard to get with a roller.

"Do you have to work tomorrow?" Ben asked as he started cutting in around the ceiling with his paintbrush. Makena followed his lead and did the same around the baseboards.

She was slow to respond to his question. His mention of work prompted thoughts of Edward, and she reminded herself to keep her mouth shut about the guy. She wanted so bad to tell Ben about him, but she couldn't.

Instead she said, "Yeah, I need to put in a few hours tomorrow."

"Have you thought anymore about joining me at my firm?" He had asked before she moved back to Cincinnati, and he continued asking every few months—as if she'd change her mind. "I promise to make sure you have Saturdays off," he added.

Makena smiled as she dipped her brush into the paint pan. "As tempting as that sounds, my answer is still no. Ben, I already told you. I don't want us mixing business with personal."

"And I told you that it wouldn't be a problem. We don't have an estate attorney, and I'd love to have you on my team."

"I don't have to work in your office to be on your team. I'll always be here for you."

He climbed down from the ladder. "And that's why I'll always—"

"Don't." Makena held up her paintbrush. "Don't say it. I already know." For a person who rarely showed or expressed emotion, he told her on more than one occasion that he loved her. He never said he was *in* love with her, but the way he treated her spoke volumes.

Ben tugged the front of her T-shirt and pulled her to him before placing a sweet kiss on her cheek. "As long as you know how I feel."

Makena's insides quivered with pleasure at their closeness. "I know. Now get back to work. We have a lot to do."

"Yes, ma'am." He turned and bumped into her, and a paintbrush stain landed on the front of her shirt.

Makena gasped. "Ben! You did that on purpose!"

His eyes grew wide. "I'm…I'm sorry," he said, his lips twitching seconds before he burst out laughing. Each time Ben tried to speak, he'd howl all over again. "Sweet— sweetheart, I did not—"

"Save it!" She ran her brush down his left arm, leaving a long white streak. "Now, we're even."

Ben's mouth dropped open. "Oh, no, we're not!"

Makena screamed when his arm snaked around her waist. "Don't you dare!" she yelled, and wiggled against him, trying to get out of his tight hold as he added globs of paint to her shirt and ratty jeans. "Ben! I can*not* believe you. Oh, man. It's on now!"

They wrestled for each other's paintbrushes as paint landed everywhere but on the walls. Before Makena realized it, they were rolling around on the plastic that was covering the floor. Her glass-shattering shrieks filled the space, and she couldn't remember the last time she'd laughed so hard.

"*Stop!*" she giggled, struggling to catch her breath as she squirmed beneath him, still tagging him with paint. "Ben! St—stop!" She couldn't stop laughing as tears blurred her vision.

"You stop, because I'm not stopping until you let go of your weapon," he huffed, trying to dodge the paintbrush in her hand. He finally got hold of her wrist and shook it. "Drop it!"

"Okay, okay, okay. I quit," Makena wheezed, dropping the brush. Laying on her back, chest heaving and arms and legs spread wide, she stared up at the ceiling feeling as if she had just gone ten rounds with Evander Holyfield. Ben laid down beside her, his breaths coming in short spurts. The room was a mess, but Makena couldn't deny that painting each other had been way more fun than painting the walls.

"I'm too old for painting." Ben gasped for air and felt

around on the floor until he found her hand. He linked his fingers with hers. "I'll call BJ in the morning."

There was no way Makena was going to argue. She should've gone with his idea in the first place. "Deal. I'll pay whatever he charges. Now, how about that banana pudding?"

*

Hours later, Ben slowly opened his eyes. The few remaining embers in the fireplace were now ash, and the television was the only thing illuminating the cozy living room. He glanced down at the top of Makena's head. She was sound asleep against his chest. How many times had he awakened like this?

This was how most of their movie nights ended up—the television watching *them*.

Makena had barely made it through the opening scene of the action flick before she started nodding off. Ben didn't mind, it gave him an excuse to pull her close. This was what he wanted all the time. After his divorce, he vowed never to get seriously involved with a woman. Sure, he'd had his share of female companionship, but no one who made him want to share his life with them. Nothing like what he and Makena shared.

Ben gave her a slight shake. "Mac, sweetheart, wake up so you can get in bed." He called her name several times before she spoke.

"I'm not asleep," she said groggily and didn't move.

"Do you want me to carry you to bed?" Ben asked, half joking.

She bolted upright. "I'm awake."

He laughed and shook his head, knowing that would wake her up.

Makena threw off the light blanket covering them and stood. It had taken them forever to clean the paint off of themselves. Ben always loved spending time with her, but wrestling around when they were supposed to be painting, had been a blast. All of the stresses of the week had fallen away and allowed them to turn into two big kids. It turned out to be a fun, but exhausting, evening. A good exhaustion, though.

Ben's body stirred when Makena stretched and her shirt lifted, revealing her almost-flat stomach. She wasn't thin or fat, but had just enough meat on her bones to entice him. He still remembered the first time he realized his feelings for her had changed.

They were meeting up at a networking event, and she'd been running late. Ben had been anxious for her arrival, and when she eventually showed up, his breath had caught in his throat. He'd seen her dressed up plenty of times, but there had been something different about her that night. Something so soul-stirringly powerful that at that moment, he no longer saw her as his best friend.

He saw her as the woman he had fallen in love with.

"Are you staying the night?" Makena asked, bringing him back to the present.

"Is that an invitation?"

She jammed her hands onto her hips and narrowed her eyes. "Let me rephrase that. It's late. You're welcome to use the guest room."

Ben stood and moved closer, sliding his arm around her waist. Instead of pulling away the way he expected, Makena leaned into him, her head resting on his chest.

"What if I want to stay in your room?"

She lifted her head and pursed her lips. "Fine. I'll sleep in the guest room." After placing a quick kiss on his cheek, she started to pull away, but Ben held tight. She fit perfectly in his arms and he loved having her softness hugged up against him.

When she gazed up at him, he brushed the back of his fingers down her cheek. "We've shared a bed in the past. Why can't we now?"

He knew why, but he wanted to hear her response. During their undergrad, when they attended college in different cities, occasionally they'd visit each other. He'd either camp out on the floor or share her bed. Their relationship had always been platonic.

Today was different.

Ben was more than ready to cross that invisible line that would lead to a romantic connection. He knew she wanted the same thing, but fear kept her from giving in to her feelings.

"How long are we going to keep doing this?" he asked.

"How long are you going to keep pushing?"

Ben smiled. "You know I'm relentless when it comes to something...or someone I want. Life is short, sweetheart. I know our feelings are mutual, but you're letting fear keep you from having the type of relationship we both want. Why not give us a shot and see what happens?"

Makena huffed out a breath and gently pushed against his chest until he released her. "And risk ruining our friendship? No, thank you. I did that with Preston."

"I'm not Preston. What you and I have is different than what you had with your ex."

"True, but..." She nibbled on her bottom lip, and her brown-eyed gaze studied him. "What if we destroy what we have?"

"We won't," Ben said with confidence, believing they were destined to be together. He reached for her, but she stepped back. "Makena."

"Ben...go to bed." She turned and walked toward the stairs that led to the bedrooms. "Oh, and I changed my mind."

His heart leaped with excitement in his chest. "About?"

"Our sleeping arrangement." Her smile turned wicked. "I have dibs on the master bedroom. I'm sure you'll be comfortable in the guest room. Have a good night."

Ben chuckled and watched her ascent up the stairs. "You know you're wrong for that," he called out. Despite her tossing him in the guest room, he wasn't discouraged.

She'll be mine one day.

It was only a matter of time.

Chapter Three

The next morning, Makena showered and slipped into a sweatshirt and yoga pants. Even though it was Saturday, and she didn't need to be in the office until later in the afternoon, she hadn't planned to sleep past ten. The enticing aroma of strong coffee, cinnamon, and something equally delicious-smelling crept up the stairs to her bedroom.

She had no choice but to get up and satisfy her foggy brain and grumbling stomach. The scents filling the air lured Makena from her bedroom and to the stairs. She cooked often. Yet, there was just something about when Ben cooked. The creations he prepared in her kitchen always made her mouth water.

One thing about snagging a Jenkins man—you were guaranteed to get a guy who could cook his butt off.

Makena's breath caught and she stopped dead in the middle of the staircase. *Snagging a Jenkins man.* The words bounced around in her mind. What was wrong with her? She couldn't be thinking of Ben that way.

They were friends.

That's it.

Nothing more.

Staring at the remaining stairs, Makena debated with herself. Should she turn around and slink back to her bedroom until he left? No. She wasn't a wimp. This was a situation that needed to be dealt with head-on. The problem was, she and Ben spent too much time together. The line between *friends* and *something more* was starting to blur. All she had to do was figure out a way to hang out without lusting after him.

But how?

Frustrated with herself and the situation, Makena marched down the remaining stairs. The sooner she sent Ben on his way, the sooner she could get her head back on straight.

She turned the corner and headed to the kitchen, but her thoughts froze inside her brain. Ben stood at the counter, pouring two mugs of coffee. That wasn't what gave her pause, though. No, it was the way his dress shirt hung open revealing a muscular chest, a hint of the FEARLESS tattoo he'd gotten while in college, and six-pack abs.

Makena had seen him shirtless before, but right now it was as if she was seeing him for the first time. An unexpected thrill coursed through her and nipped at every nerve inside her body.

This is not good.

No way should she be looking at him with the hunger of a bear that hadn't eaten in months. But she couldn't help it. The man was near perfect in every way possible.

To her displeasure, Ben started buttoning his shirt and stopped after one button. Makena wasn't sure if she made a noise, but his gaze shot to her. She tried keeping her eyes on his face. It was no use. Her attention kept drifting to the expanse of chest still on display.

Ben grinned as if knowing where her thoughts had taken her. "Good morning. I was just about to bring you a cup of coffee."

"Morning," she mumbled, trying not to look at him as he closed a few more buttons before handing her the steaming brew. "Did you sleep okay?"

"Yeah, but I could've slept better if you were lying next

to me."

Makena narrowed her eyes and gave him a *don't start* look as she brought the coffee mug to her mouth.

Ben chuckled, clearly reading her thoughts. "Okay, I'll drop it for now. I made pancakes and sausage, but I wasn't sure when you'd be up."

As Makena watched him move across the kitchen, she took a careful sip of the steaming coffee.

Perfect.

Strong brew with two sugars and a dash of cream was just how she liked it, and Ben made it perfectly every time.

He went to the wall ovens and pulled open the warming drawer beneath the bottom one. When Makena had her kitchen remodeled the year before, there were some luxuries she had insisted on. The double ovens, five-burner stove with a griddle, and the warming drawer were a few of those items. The kitchen wasn't as large as she would've liked, but what it lacked in size, it made up for in function.

Her stomach growled when she glanced down at the plate Ben set in front of her. The enticing aroma hijacked her senses and had her mouth watering. She hated when her foods touched, and though her plate was full, none of the items touched. Sometimes it was scary how well Ben knew her. He had prepared her favorite—cinnamon bun pancakes. There was also sausage, and he had even cut up bell peppers and onions in the hash browns just the way she liked. Lastly, he set a small bowl with a grapefruit sliced in four sections next to the plate.

"Oh, my goodness, Ben. You're going to spoil me."

"That's my plan." He walked around the breakfast bar with his coffee and sat next to her.

"Aren't you going to eat?" Makena asked around a forkful of hash browns.

"I ate a little bit earlier." He settled on the bar stool next to her and took a careful sip of his coffee. "Do you have plans next Saturday night?"

Makena narrowed her eyes. "So this little feast is meant

to butter me up for something?"

Ben chuckled and pushed a strand of her hair behind her ear as if it was the most natural thing in the world to do. The intimate gesture sent heat rushing through Makena's body.

"You know I love cooking for you. If I was trying to butter you up for something, I would've come with jewelry or plane tickets to someplace exotic."

Now she was the one laughing because he probably would've.

"So what's happening next Saturday?" she asked, cutting into her pancakes.

The moment the sweetness hit her tongue, her eyes rolled to the back of her head. A moan slipped out before Makena could stop it.

"These are sooo good." She didn't bother looking at Ben. She could practically feel him grinning and sticking his chest out.

"I'm glad you like them. Now, about Saturday. I need you to be my plus-one for a fundraiser."

Makena listened as he told her about the group that was raising money for the new community center. For as long as she'd known Ben, he'd been involved in various projects and nonprofits around the city. As Makena watched Ben speak animatedly about the community center, her time with Edward Foxall came to mind.

Identical eyes.

Same facial expressions.

Similar mannerisms.

She had to figure out a way for him and Ben to meet. But how could she do that and still remain ethical?

"Makena?"

Her gaze shot to Ben. "I'm sorry, what?"

His brows dipped into a frown. "You okay? Where'd you go?"

"I was just thinking…" she started, debating on what to say. "I have a client who reminds me of you."

"Oh, yeah? What—he's good-looking, brilliant, and crazy

about a certain estate attorney?"

Makena rolled her eyes. "Yeah, something like that. Anyway, back to the fundraiser. Is it formal?"

"It is. Will that be a problem?"

"Nope, it's been a while since I dressed up. I'm looking forward to it."

"Great, then it's a date."

Makena's fork stopped inches from her mouth. Hadn't she just told herself that she had to put distance between them? Now here Ben was, calling the fundraiser a date.

"Just stop," he said with force, and Makena looked at him.

"What?"

"Don't overthink this outing. I know you're against us *dating*, but I need a date that night, and you're the only person I want to attend with. Okay?"

Makena huffed out a breath and nodded. Maybe she was overthinking their relationship and how it was transforming. But who could blame her? The man was super *fine*, intelligent, and one of the sexiest men she knew.

At her age, she didn't run across men like him; a real man. A man who adored his family. A man who was dependable and didn't run from responsibilities. A man any woman would be proud to call her own.

It scared Makena to death to admit that she had it bad for him.

They chatted while she ate. It didn't matter how much time they spent together, they always found something to talk about.

That had been one of several problems with her and Preston. Conversation stopped. He was an amazing father, but Makena learned early on that they shouldn't have gotten married. They were too much alike and not necessarily in the best way. They started growing apart and barely tolerated each other. Though it might not have been the best idea, they had stayed together for their daughter. Maintaining a stable home-front for her had been their number one goal.

Once Ava was in high school, Makena and Preston separated. Soon after that, they divorced. Makena was grateful that their split had been amicable and quick. Though Preston still lived in Columbus, approximately an hour car ride away, he was very active in Ava's life. Makena couldn't ask for more than that.

She finished her meal and rubbed her stomach. "That was excellent. Thanks again for breakfast."

"Anything for you, sweetness." Ben stood, grabbed her empty plate and his mug and carried them to the sink.

"The least I can do is clean up," Makena said, and started rinsing dishes and placing them in the dishwasher.

"I need to get going." Ben leaned against the counter next to her. "I have to go home before I head into the office. What does your day look like?"

"Same as you. I have some work at the office, then I'm coming home. Ava is coming by tonight to do laundry. I figured I'd cook dinner and hang out with her," she said of her daughter who attended the University of Cincinnati.

Ben nodded and watched Makena with an intensity she couldn't decipher. She turned to him fully and placed her hand on her hip.

"What's that look for?"

He shook his head. "Nothing. I just like looking at you."

Makena studied him, not sure what to say to that. She loved looking at him, too, and it scared her. She and Preston had been good friends while attending the same college, but once they'd gotten married, things changed. Makena refused to make that same mistake with Ben, but what she felt for him was so much stronger than what it had been when she was with Preston.

"Come here." Ben pulled her close.

Makena didn't protest. Instead she wrapped her arms around his neck and placed her chin on his shoulder. She might be afraid to risk their friendship for something more serious, but there was one thing she couldn't deny. Being in Ben's strong arms felt like home. Warm. Comfortable. Safe. It felt right. *He* felt right.

She inhaled his fresh scent, a combination of his natural redolence and the body wash in the guest bathroom. Makena loved everything about this man. He was intelligent, kind, honorable, and the most dependable man she knew. He was everything she desired. What if she was making a mistake by not taking their relationship to the next level? What if she kept the distance between them, and another woman came along and snagged his attention? She would never know if they could be more than friends if she didn't give them a chance.

No. No. No, her common sense screamed inside of her. *I can't. We can't*, she told herself.

Ben moved slightly, and Makena's head shot up. Their gazes collided, and before she could process what was happening, his mouth settled over hers. The realization that he was…that she was…that they were kissing each other, hit Makena like a two-by-four against her head.

The kiss was urgent, yet exploratory. She knew she should stop what he had started. She knew she should push him away. She even knew the last thing they should be doing was kissing. But man if she wasn't enjoying the moment.

The kiss quickly grew more intense, sending the pit of her stomach into a tailspin. Ben's hold on her tightened and he deepened their connection. Makena's brain told her to back away, but the desire pulsing through her body said *no, not yet*.

"Well, it's about time."

Ben and Makena startled apart like two teenagers getting caught making out in the back seat of a car. She tried catching her breath as her heart practically pounded out of her chest and her hand hovered over her mouth.

Her daughter Ava stood at the opening of the kitchen, grinning like she was just notified that she had won *Publishers Clearing House Sweepstakes*.

"Does that mean that you approve?" Ben asked, his grin matching Ava's.

Makena swatted his arm as embarrassment swirled inside of her. "There's nothing to approve. That ki— Uh, this," she stammered, shocked that she hadn't heard her daughter enter the house. "This is not what it looked like."

Ava burst out laughing. "Well, it looked like a whole lotta something to me." She strolled toward them, still grinning and walked into Ben's arms, greeting him with a hug like usual. "Hey, Uncle Ben. Are those your famous pancakes I smell?" she asked, searching the kitchen.

"Yeah, there's plenty left in the warming drawer. Help yourself. We've eaten."

Ava's gaze bounced from Ben to Makena. "Really? 'Cause you guys still look a little *hungry* to me." She burst out laughing again and this time Ben joined in.

Makena growled under her breath and glared at him. "Don't you have somewhere to be?" she snapped, without much bite in her tone. She never could stay mad at him. "Out!"

Still chuckling, Ben reached for her hand and pulled her toward the front of the house. "I'm not sorry about the kiss," he said and sat on the bench in the foyer and slipped on his shoes. "No matter how much you fight our attraction, we're destined to be together."

Makena didn't say anything as he continued giving his closing argument, addressing all the reasons why they were already more than friends. She could barely focus on what he was saying. Her mind was too consumed with the fact that they had kissed, seriously kissed.

And she liked it.

A lot.

By the time she zoned back into their conversation, Ben had his suit jacket on and his overcoat in his arms.

His hand slid to the back of her neck and her pulse pounded in her ears as he pulled her close. Instead of a repeat of the kiss they'd just shared moments ago, he placed a lingering kiss on her forehead.

"Try not to overthink what happened, all right?"

Makena nodded, knowing that's exactly what she was going to do. It was her nature to obsess about everything.

"I'll call you later."

"Okay." Makena locked the door behind him and stood in the foyer, still trying to come to terms with the shift in their relationship.

"Mom!" Ava yelled from the kitchen. "Do you have any peanut butter?"

Makena strolled back into the kitchen, and that stupid grin was back on her daughter's face.

"Don't say anything," Makena instructed, not wanting to talk about Ben. She pulled an unopened jar of peanut butter out of the pantry and handed it to Ava.

"Does that mean you don't want to talk about how you were sucking face with Uncle Ben?" Ava asked with a straight face, until her lips started twitching. She looked away and proceeded to spread peanut butter on top of the already-sweet pancakes.

She and Ava had a wonderful relationship where they could discuss practically anything. Makena just wasn't sure she wanted to discuss Ben with her.

"Come on, Mom. Don't be embarrassed. I'm actually glad you guys are more than friends."

"We're not more than friends," Makena said defensively.

"Seriously? That kiss said otherwise." Ava cut into her pancakes, then moaned. "Man, these are as good as I remember." She ate a little more before speaking again. "I don't know what the big deal is. If you like Uncle Ben and he likes you, I say go for it. They say friends make the best lovers."

"Excuse me?" Makena propped her hand on her hip. "What do you know about friends and lovers?"

"Come on, Mom. I'm in college. I know things." She wiggled her eyebrows, and Makena cringed at the route the conversation was going. She trusted her daughter to make good decisions, but there were some things she just didn't want to know.

Makena sighed and poured herself another cup of coffee. "I'm crazy about Ben, and he's my best friend. I don't want to do anything to mess that up. I don't want us to cross that line and ruin what we have."

"I think it's too late for that," Ava cracked, that goofy grin plastered on her face again, but then she turned serious. "Have you ever thought about why the guys you've gone on dates with don't measure up?"

"Probably because I'm out of practice and need a tutorial in dating."

Ava laughed. "No, it's because Uncle Ben is *it* for you. Sometimes you can't fight what's destined to be, and you guys are so cute together. Since we moved back to Cincinnati, it's clear that there's something special between you and Uncle Ben. I think maybe there always has been."

Makena shook her head. "It would be too weird for us to date."

"How would it be any different? When you're not working or hanging out with me or Halle, you're with him. You talk about him all the time like he's your man. The only difference in officially dating him would be adding sex to the equation."

"Stop right there. What did I tell you when I gave you *the talk*? No sex before marriage."

"Oh, yeah. *Riii-ght*," her daughter said, nodding her head and looking at Makena as if to say, *you just keep thinking that*. "Anyway, I think you should give Uncle Ben a chance."

"I don't know," was all Makena could say. She loved Ben, there was no denying that, but...

"Aren't you the one who's always telling me to not let fear rule my life? Maybe it's time you took your own advice. I would hate for you to miss out on a good thing because you're scared."

Makena studied her daughter, the love of her life, and smiled. She wrapped her arms around her in a tight hug. "When did you get so smart?"

"Oh, I don't know. I'm thinking I've always been like

this. And for the record, I approve of you and Uncle Ben. He's pretty hot for an old guy."

Makena burst out laughing. "Yeah, he really is."

Maybe it was time to practice what she preached. Fear could have her missing out on the one man who set her body on fire.

Ben was right about one thing. Life was short.

It was time she started living, and what better way to do that than with him?

Chapter Four

"Jealousy is not a good look on you."

Makena's attention snapped to Ben's sister, Carolyn. "I have no idea what you're talking about," she said, her cheeks heating at the blatant lie.

Carolyn bumped shoulders with her and laughed. "Yeah, tell it to someone who doesn't know you. The daggers shooting from your eyes are a dead giveaway."

Makena had never known herself to be the jealous type, but since arriving at the fundraiser, she'd been protective of Ben. She hated the way some of the women in attendance were getting in his face and vying for his attention. Even now, she watched from across the ballroom as another woman approached him.

When Makena and Ben first arrived, he'd kept her close, which was fine with her. They'd been side by side for much of the fundraiser, but after dinner and the program, he'd been pulled away from the table. As one of the featured business men for the event, it was understandable that people were anxious to talk to him. He had also won a much-deserved award for his community service, and everyone was eager to congratulate him.

Still, Makena hated the way some of the women blatantly threw themselves at him. She couldn't much blame them. The midnight-blue tuxedo with black lapels sheathed his fit body, bringing attention to his wide shoulders and narrow waist. Combine those qualities with his good looks, gorgeous smile, and charming personality, and he stood out from all the other men in the room.

"You and my brother are a trip," Carolyn cracked, shaking her head and smiling.

Makena pulled her attention from Ben and turned to his sister. Carolyn might have been a couple of years older than Makena, but growing up, they were good friends. Nights like tonight, they often gravitated to each other. They had just returned from the ladies' room, but had been stopped by the mayor's wife, a big talker. At some point, Makena had tuned out of the conversation, and now realized the other woman had moved on.

"What do you mean?" Makena asked.

"I mean you two can't take your eyes off of each other. I know you were trying to give him space to circulate, but you might as well go on back over there."

"I don't want to come across as clingy."

Carolyn waved her off. "Oh please. No one could ever accuse you of being clingy. If anything, it's the other way around. He hasn't let you out of his sight, probably because of that dress."

Makena glanced down at her evening gown. After debating between two outfits, she had decided on a shimmering silver dress with sheer sleeves and a long V that stopped at the swell of her breasts. Ben's sudden intake of breath when he picked her up earlier was all the assurance she'd needed to know that she had made the right choice. And his eyes had practically bugged out of his head when he spotted the long split that revealed her left leg whenever she moved. The outfit was bolder than she normally wore, but his reaction had made her feel like a goddess.

"Hey, Auntie and Mac, we're getting ready to leave."

Makena turned to Nate, Ben's nephew, and his wife Liberty. They were such an adorable couple. After being college sweethearts, they were abruptly torn apart. It seemed unlikely that they would ever find their way back to each other; not until fate stepped in a couple of years ago. Despite the rocky reunion, they were now married, with twin one-year-old boys.

Liberty was an associate lawyer at Ben's law firm, and Nate, the CFO for Jenkins & Sons Construction, worked with Ben as well. They had partnered a couple of years earlier and started a property development company. Makena didn't know how any of them juggled their busy schedules.

"We have to go and relieve the babysitter. I'm sure the twins have probably worn her out by now," Liberty said, referring to their boys.

"Well, it was good seeing you both." Makena hugged Liberty. "What happened to Nick and Sumeera?" She just realized that everyone had vacated the table they'd all shared earlier.

"Oh, they're still here somewhere. We'll probably run into them in the hallway," Nate said, giving Makena a hug. "We'll see you soon, and tell Uncle Ben I'll catch him later."

"I will."

"Okay, you're up," Carolyn said to Makena and nodded toward Ben who was now talking to a woman wearing a seductive red evening gown. "That's Sydney. She's been trying to get her claws into Ben for years. I suggest you go over and run interference."

"I think you're right. I saw her earlier. She tried snagging Ben's attention when we first arrived, but he managed to dodge her. I'll go over and introduce myself."

"You do that, and I'm gonna go and rescue my husband. He's been holding court with those men long enough. They're probably asking for free financial advice." Her husband, Lincoln Richwood, was a financial adviser and seemed to know practically everyone in attendance.

Makena hugged Carolyn and then moved further into the ballroom. Now was actually the perfect time to rejoin Ben since the band had started back up after a short break. She loved dancing, though she didn't get to do it often.

She maneuvered around several round tables. Dinner and the program had ended twenty minutes ago, but people were still sitting around and talking.

The organizers had done a beautiful job with the lavishly decorated ballroom. They had gone with a light blue, brown, and various shades of gray color scheme. The tablecloths were gray, and the chair coverings were gray with a brown sash. Blue accents, including cloth napkins and blue LED uplighting, transformed the walls and gave the room an elegant pop of color.

But it was the intricate floral centerpieces that pulled everything together. Extra-tall crystal vases were on the tables, making it easy for guests to still communicate without obstructing their view. The lovely floral arrangement consisted of blue irises, white orchids, and strings of pearls dripping down the side of the vases.

When Makena glanced at Ben again, he was staring at her. His heated gaze seeped into her and burned a path straight to her core. How could just a look spark something so passionately powerful within her?

And then he smiled.

Goodness.

A sweet thrill shot through her body, and she picked up her pace. She couldn't wait to be in his arms.

Sydney glanced over her shoulder. At first, a smile was perched on her ruby-red lips, but it dropped when she spotted Makena headed their way.

"I was just about to come get you," Ben said, pulling Makena to his side and placing a lingering kiss on her temple. "Makena, this is Sydney. She's with the county treasurer's office. Sydney, this is my date, Makena Nichols."

"Hello," Makena greeted with a nod.

Sydney gave her a quick once-over. "Hello. I haven't seen you before. Are you new to this area?"

Makena slid her arm around Ben's waist and leaned into him. It was about time she staked her claim. "No, I grew up here." She looked up at Ben. "I'm sorry to interrupt you two, but how about that dance?"

"I'm all yours, sweetheart. Have a good evening, Sydney," Ben said. With her hand in his, he guided Makena around a few tables and to the dance floor. She hadn't missed the scowl on Sydney's face, but she didn't care. If anyone was going to spend the rest of the evening with Ben, it was going to be her.

"Thanks for coming to my rescue," he whispered close to her ear, arousing a desire within her that he had stoked throughout the night.

She smiled at him. "Any time."

When they reached the dance floor, Ben lifted Makena's hand up over her head and then spun her before pulling her into his arms. Hugged up to his hard body, she was so glad the band was playing a slow song. Not that she needed an excuse to get close to him.

Ben held one of Makena's hand to his chest and her other arm went around his neck as their bodies swayed to the smooth melody. If she hadn't seen the singer, Makena would've thought India Arie herself was on stage singing her song, "Steady Love."

"Have I mentioned how much I love your dress?"

"You might have mentioned it a few times. I'm glad you like it."

He nuzzled the area behind her ear and delicious tingles elicited a soft moan from her. This man had the ability to turn her body to butter if she didn't maintain some control.

"So…you and Sydney, huh?" she asked as casually as she could. Considering how close the woman had been standing to him, Makena couldn't help wondering if they'd been an item at some point.

Ben slowed and leaned his head back, meeting Makena's gaze. "Me and Sydney what?"

Mindful that the dance floor was filling up, she kept her voice low. "Are you…or were you two an item?"

"No. Never. Next question," he said with amusement.

"Wait. Don't tell me you were jealous."

She could lie, but why bother? "Maybe a little."

"Don't be. I've never been interested in her, and I never will be. There's only one woman I want."

Makena's heart fluttered inside of her chest and a surge of arousal pulsed through her veins. He was such a sweet talker. Then again, he was so much more than that. He was hers if she wanted him.

She caressed the back of his head as she stared into his sexy eyes, loving the intimacy of dancing with him. "I'm glad to hear that. Because if you and I are going to date, you need to make it clear to your admirers that you're no longer available."

Ben stopped in the middle of the dance floor. "Are you saying what I think you're saying?"

Makena bit back a smile. "I thought I was pretty clear."

Ben laughed, and he cupped her face between his hands as he searched her eyes. The gentleness of the way he was brushing the pad of his thumbs over her cheeks made Makena's heart melt a little.

"I'll be happy to shout it to the world that I'm all yours, and what better way to make that clear than by doing this."

He lowered his head and captured her mouth in a hot, sensual kiss, one that was full of love and promises. His hands moved from her face. One slid behind her neck and the other around her waist as he held her tight to him.

Makena pushed everything and everybody from her mind and got swept away by the intensity of the kiss. Their kiss the week before had been mind-numbing, but this…this one was like no other. Cushioned against his muscular body, she felt all of him, even the hardness of his shaft pressing against her stomach.

A wave of desire crashed through her, and she gripped the back of Ben's suit jacket when her knees went weak. She had wondered if the kiss last week had been a fluke.

It hadn't been.

Kissing Ben was like an awakening of all her senses. Why

had she protested them crossing that line?

Nothing that feels this good could be wrong, she thought. If only she hadn't been afraid, they could've been experiencing this connection much sooner.

When they finally came up for air, Makena noticed the band was playing a different song. Glancing around the crowded dance floor, she also realized they had snagged the attention of some of the other guests. A woman a few feet away smiled and gave her a thumbs-up.

Makena's face heated. She had never been into public displays of affection and kissing a man in the middle of a dance floor was a first. Even in her fifties, she had a feeling that she'd have a lot of firsts with Ben.

He caressed her cheek. "You won't regret taking a chance on me," he said quietly, and Makena assumed he was talking about the new status of their relationship. "You and I are meant to be together."

He'd said that to her on more than one occasion over the last few months. Suddenly, Makena believed him. She knew early on in her marriage that she had married the wrong man. She just never considered that Ben might've been the man for her.

Ben lowered his hand and reached for hers. "Why don't we get out of here?"

"That sounds like a good idea."

Chapter Five

Excitement thumped through Ben as he maneuvered his SUV through the streets of Cincinnati. He only wished he had gone with his initial idea of getting a driver for the evening. Holding Makena's hand now, while still feeling that kiss that they shared on the dance floor, was making it hard to focus on the road.

It was official.

They were a couple.

She was his.

He knew at some point she would come around to his way of thinking and discover what he'd known for a long time. They were destined to be together. Ben just hadn't expected her to acknowledge that truth in the middle of a dance floor.

During the past week, there had been signs that she was ready to take their friendship to the next level.

Since that kiss in her kitchen, they spent almost every evening together. He made it a point to stop by her place, if only for a few minutes, on his way home. Makena hadn't deflected any of his subtle moves. Holding her hand. A touch here and there. A kiss on the lips when greeting her, and another when they went their separate ways.

He especially knew something was up when he picked

her up for the fundraiser, and she'd handed him her overnight bag.

"I'm so proud of you," Makena said out of the blue.

Ben split his attention between her and the road as he hopped on I-71 North toward his home. He thought she would continue, but she went quiet.

"Okaay. What'd I do?"

"The award you received," she said as if he should've known what she was thinking. "It's wonderful that no matter how crazy your schedule is, you still find time to do volunteer work. You're not only generous with your time, but also your money."

Emotion swelled inside of Ben at her kind words. It was one thing to make your parents, or even your kids proud. It was something altogether different when the love of your life said that she was proud of you.

"Thank you. That means a lot to hear you say that." Actually, it meant more then he'd ever be able to express. "When I was in law school, I had vowed that once I had a little money and influence, I was going to invest in the community I grew up in."

Makena nodded. "I think I'm going to start getting more involved. Maybe you can help me decide where to begin."

"Actually, the new community center is in need of math tutors. You interested? It'll require at least a two-hour-per-week commitment."

"I think I can handle that." She glanced down at their joined hands and nibbled on her bottom lip. "So, now that we're dating, where do we go from here?"

Ben brought her hand to his mouth and kissed the back of her fingers. "To be honest, I'm not sure. All I know is that I want to spend as much time with you as possible. Mac, I'm not taking what you and I have lightly, and you need to know that this is not just a fling for me."

"I know that, and I feel the same way. We already spend more time together than most married couples, but I'm sure there are still things we don't know about each other."

"True. I guess now we'll focus on getting to know each other on a different level."

*

Twenty-five minutes later, Makena's nerves were on high alert as Ben let them into his home. She wasn't nervous to spend time with him, but her thoughts were going a mile a minute. What happened next? She was spending the night. Would he expect them to be intimate? Did she want them to be intimate?

Yes and no, said the tiny voice inside her head.

Yes, because she was curious. If Ben was as good in bed as he was with every other aspect of his life, it would be a night to remember.

No, because once they crossed that line and made love, there was no going back. Their relationship would be forever changed. They wouldn't only be dating. They would also be lovers.

Was she ready for that?

If she was honest with herself, the answer was yes. She just had to stop thinking so much and live in the moment.

As she strolled through the mudroom and into the kitchen, some of the tension left her body. She loved Ben's house. It was a place that felt just as much like home as hers did.

The ranch-style home, with almost three thousand square feet, had four bedrooms, four bathrooms, and sat on almost two acres. Normally, Makena was partial to open floor plans, but the majority of the home was closed off. The exception was the kitchen, which opened up to a large family room; that was mainly where they hung out. On occasion they'd sit in the formal living room or use the formal dining room, but that was rare.

"You already know to make yourself at home," Ben said from behind her as he reset the house alarm.

He headed in the direction of the bedrooms, carrying her overnight case as well as his duffel bag. He had probably originally planned to stay the night at her place. That was until she had handed him her bag when he picked her up. The surprised look on his face had been comical, and Makena was glad she could still surprise him.

She roamed through the house, her heels clicking on the oak hardwood floors. Considering Ben wasn't conservative with his ideas or his style of dress, his home decor was traditional. The dark, masculine furniture with wood accents was comfortable looking with splashes of colors all around.

Makena made her way back to the kitchen and stopped at the sliding glass patio door. She stared out at the deck that overlooked a huge fenced-in yard. There was a pool and a play set that some of the Jenkins men built for Ben's five-year-old grandson. The imposing structure stood out and included a fort, swings, a slide, and a climbing wall.

Ben returned to the kitchen and Makena watched him through the reflection in the window as he approached.

"You doing okay?" he asked.

"Oh, yeah. Seems as if I haven't been here in like forever."

"That's because you haven't. It's been a few weeks. Maybe even a month."

She lived in the city and closer to both of their jobs. It was always easier to meet up at her place after work, instead of them driving to his place.

Ben wrapped his arms around her from behind, and nuzzled her neck. "In the car, on our way here, I mentioned that I would follow your lead here on out."

Makena couldn't stop the smile that spread across her lips. She knew he meant that when he'd said it, but she also knew it was only a matter of time before he took the lead.

"Yeah," she said, dragging the one word out while wondering where he was going with the conversation.

"There's one thing that's non-negotiable." He placed a sweet, sensual kiss behind her ear, and a tingle of pleasure shot through her body, down to the soles of her feet. "I won't be flexible when it comes to where you sleep when you're here."

Makena slowly turned in his arms and faced him. Her lips twitched as she fingered his bowtie. "Is that right?"

"Yep. Non-negotiable."

She gave a little shrug. "That's fine since I'm planning to sleep wherever you do."

Ben's gorgeous eyes narrowed, and he remained quiet as if waiting for her to say more. Makena could admit to giving him a hard time occasionally, but not in this case. They wanted the same thing.

"Quit looking at me like that," she said, slowly undoing his bowtie. "You're not going to get an argument from me regarding sleeping arrangements."

His brows shot up. "No?"

"No. Like you, I'm all in. Your speech the other morning about life being too short resonated with me." She tugged the tie from around his neck and tossed it on the kitchen counter. Then she started on the top buttons of his shirt.

It had been a long time since Makena had been with a man, and she couldn't think of anyone she wanted more than she wanted Ben.

"Besides, I'm tired of fighting my feelings for you," she continued, the nervousness from earlier subsiding. "I want to see where this goes, and you promised that our friendship won't be in jeopardy. I'm holding you to that promise."

Ben nodded. "Me, too."

With an arm around her waist, he pulled her against his hard body and covered her mouth with his. That kiss on the dance floor had stirred a passion within Makena that she hadn't felt in ages, and this one was no different. Being with Ben like this felt natural, and everything about the moment felt right.

"I love kissing you," he mumbled against her lips before lifting his head and staring into Makena's eyes. "But I want more."

She cupped his cheek and with the pad of her thumb, wiped her lipstick from his lips. "Then what are you waiting for?"

Chapter Six

"You sure about this?" Ben asked.

They were in his dimly lit bedroom, and Makena ran her sweaty palms down her sides, trying not to fidget under his intense perusal.

"I'm not going to lie. I'm a little nervous, but I'm sure. I want to be with you in every way possible."

Ben removed his scales of justice cuff links that Makena had given him for Christmas and set them in a tray on top of his dresser. As he undid the remaining buttons on his shirt, he continued watching her, as if trying to figure out if she was having second thoughts.

Little did he know, she had often thought about them getting together. Yes, it was a little weird seeing her friend undress in front of her and wanting him like she wanted no other man. But the love and respect Makena had for him outshone any awkwardness.

Shrugging out of his tuxedo shirt, Ben tossed it into a nearby chair. That left him in a fitted white T-shirt that stretched across his wide chest.

As he closed the short distance between them, the love gleaming in his sexy eyes matched what Makena felt deep inside her soul. They were right where they were supposed to be. Moments from now, she would be his in every way possible.

He stopped in front of her, leaving only inches between them, and Makena swallowed hard. An anxious anticipation snaked through her body. They were doing this. They were taking their relationship to the next level. Everything would change from here on out.

Ben cradled her face between his large hands and stared into her eyes. The tenderness in his expression, and the soothing way he caressed her cheek, almost made her whimper. This tough-as-nails lawyer was one of the gentlest men she knew, and he was hers.

"Relax. We won't do anything you don't want to do, all right?"

Makena nodded. Even though she knew that, it still felt good to hear him say the words.

They stood there staring for what seemed like long minutes but were mere seconds, neither saying a word. It wasn't an uncomfortable silence. No. It was as if they were breathing each other in and savoring that moment in time.

Ben lowered his forehead to hers. "God, I love you," he said quietly with such deeply felt emotion. They expressed their feelings for each other all the time, throwing out *I love yous* in passing. Though Makena meant the words whenever she spoke them, and she knew he did as well, this time was different. This time his declaration stabbed her in the heart and triggered a ripple of emotion swirling inside of her.

Makena gripped the front of his T-shirt. "I love you more."

Considering she'd once been married, she couldn't ever remember experiencing this type of connection with anyone. His patience. His kindness. His ability to read her moods without a word being spoken, were only a few of Ben's attributes that she adored. Consummating this new chapter in their lives was a little scary. Yet, there was no other place Makena would rather be than right there with him.

Ben straightened. He unfastened the silver rhinestone barrette that held her hair up in an elaborate twist on top of her head. Her long tresses fell around her shoulders and a few strands covered her face. After reaching over and setting the barrette on the dresser, he ran his fingers through her hair, tenderly pushing strands out of her face.

With every move, with every sweet gesture he made, Makena's heart beat a little faster. And when he kissed her, a slow drugging kiss, fireworks shot off inside of her. He was an amazing kisser and took his time, allowing his tongue to thoroughly explore the inner recesses of her mouth.

Weak in the knees, Makena tightened her hold on his T-shirt. She was barely able to stand upright as their tongues tangled. Never had she been kissed with such love and passion, and she intended to enjoy every minute. The dizzying desire pulsing through her veins only made her more excited about their connection. Her body was on fire for him, and she was more than ready to…

Breathing hard, Ben suddenly pulled his mouth from hers. "We gotta get you out of this dress," he said roughly.

Makena was in total agreement. Holding onto him, she toed off her heels, then reached behind her to unzip her evening gown, but Ben stopped her.

"Let me get that."

She held her hair off of her neck as Ben lowered the zipper down her back. After he eased the garment off her shoulders, an involuntary shiver attacked Makena's body when air hit her bare skin.

"Are you cold?"

She shook her head and pushed the dress all the way down until it pooled around her feet.

"You sure? I can turn the heat up." His warm hands settled on her hips and he pulled her back against his hard body. She shivered again, and Ben chuckled. "Clearly, I need to turn up the heat."

He peppered soft kisses along the column of her neck as his large hands moved down her body. Makena wasn't sure if he meant turn up the heat literally or figuratively, but suddenly she was burning up inside.

"I'm fine," she rasped, then cleared her throat. Her heart pounded hard and fast enough to beat right out of her chest. Yet, she was not going to let her fears talk her out of being with the man she adored.

The man she loved.

Ben picked her dress up from the floor and laid it across a nearby chair. When he turned back to her, he froze. His hungry gaze ate her up from head to toe, devouring every inch of her body. The gray lace bra and panty set that matched her dress had been a last-minute purchase, but by his reaction, Makena was glad she had splurged. The fervor glowing in his gorgeous eyes as he took her in had her nipples hardening against the lace bra.

"Babe." His voice held so much admiration as he slowly moved back to her. "I knew you would be stunning beneath the clothes, but you're…you're absolutely breathtaking."

Makena had never been shy about her imperfect body and never needed affirmation from a man. But if she was honest with herself, Ben's words and reverence meant everything. She might've been standing in only her underwear, but she felt strong and powerful under his steady gaze.

His hand seared a path up her torso, and he slipped one arm around her waist, drawing her to him. And his other hand cupped one of her breasts.

Makena sucked in a breath and moaned as he kneaded, squeezed, and teased her nipple through the lace. Add that to the way he kissed and sucked on her neck, and she became putty in his hands. Liquid heat pulled between her thighs and desire roared through her body.

"You feel so good," he said, continuing the sweet torture by sprinkling kisses on her neck, her shoulders, and her lace-covered breasts. There was no place on her upper body that his lips didn't touch. Ben's mouth, his hands, and the feel of him against her, robbed Makena of any coherent thought. She held on to his shoulders as he continued his exploration.

"You're wearing my favorite perfume," he mumbled

against her heated skin.

Makena ached to get closer to him. "I—I didn't know you—you had a favorite."

His large hand gripped one of her butt cheeks, drawing her tight against him, and his mouth moved back up her body. "Any fragrance you wear is my favorite."

Makena laughed despite herself. Heat crackled along her nerve endings, and she squirmed against him as the light stubble on his face tickled her cheek.

"You're really pouring on the charm tonight," she panted and wiggled out of his hold, struggling to catch her breath. "Okay, okay," she pointed at him. "Your turn. Get rid of your clothes."

Ben was out of the rest of his attire in seconds, dropping them in a pile on the floor. Makena's pulse pounded in her ears as she took in his muscular physique decked out in only his boxer briefs.

"Wow." The word slipped between her lips on a whisper.

Ben wasn't big and bulky like a body builder or football player. No, he was tall, lean, and powerfully built. His body was perfectly sculpted with rippling muscles everywhere her eyes looked.

"It's a shame you hide all of..." Makena waved her hand up and down, trying to find the words that could adequately describe his magnificence. She had seen him shirtless before, but now that she was viewing the whole package... "Your body is a work of art."

Ben chuckled. "Funny, I was thinking the same about you."

She zoned in on the tattoo stamped out in bold lettering across his chest. Of all of the words he could've selected, he'd chosen FEARLESS. He had once told her that he wanted a word that, whenever he looked in the mirror, would remind him to be confident and courageous in anything he set out to do. And fearlessly was how he tackled every situation.

His smooth skin, dusted with minimum hair, beckoned

for her to touch. Makena didn't stop herself. She slid her hands up the front of his body, loving how his muscles contracted under her touch. She traced a finger over the tattoo, and Ben trembled.

"Your hands are cold."

"And your sexy body is hot enough to heat them up," she countered.

Amusement flickered in his eyes. "Look at you talking dirty. Keep that sassiness coming, but right now, I want to see all of you."

Ben reached behind her back and with a flick of his wrist, he unfastened her bra. He peeled it from her body and tossed it aside. The intensity in his gaze aroused all of her woman parts, and goosebumps skittered up her arms. He didn't have to say anything. The passion in his eyes said it all. He liked what he saw.

Those darn nerves were back, wreaking havoc on her calm, but Makena refused to let them get the best of her.

This was Ben. He might've been her best friend, but he was also the man she was crazy about. The other day, kissing him passionately for the first time weirded her out a little. But the desire that kiss evoked left her wanting more. Much more.

She had always been attracted to him, but didn't dare cross that line. Now, she couldn't think of anything she wanted more than him.

Instead of standing there like a statue on display, she slipped her fingers into the side waistband of her panties. But Ben lightly swatted her hand away.

"Not yet. Tonight, undressing you is my job. It'll be like unwrapping a Christmas present that I've been waiting forever for."

Makena sucked in a breath when he cupped her breasts, gently squeezing them as he pushed them together. "Damn, you are so..." his words trailed off, and he bent slightly and started peppering feathery kisses down her chest while brushing the pads of his thumbs across her taut nipples. "I'm taking my time so that I can sample every inch of you."

When his mouth closed around her nipple, an electric current arced within Makena and her knees went weak. *Oh my.* She gripped his shoulders, struggling to keep herself upright, as her body quivered with every lap of his tongue.

"Ben," she moaned, and her hands went to the back of his head. The pulse between her thighs throbbed with need and was almost unbearable as he continued his delicious torment. She held on, afraid if she didn't, she would puddle to the floor.

"Now, let's get you out of these." He fingered her panties, then placed a kiss just above the waistband. A tingling sensation shot through Makena's body to the soles of her feet.

Sliding the material down her legs, Ben helped her step out of them, then added them to the pile of clothing on the floor.

"I've wanted to see you like this for a long time," he said, his voice thick with desire as he straightened to his full six foot height.

He started to back her up to the bed, but Makena stopped him. "Your turn," she said calmer than what she was feeling and nodded at his black boxer briefs.

Inside, every nerve in her body was on high alert. She might've fantasized about them coming together like this, but she never thought it would actually happen.

Lust shot through her veins as Ben slipped out of his underwear and added it to the growing pile of clothes.

Wow, that small voice inside of her head said with awe. There was just enough light for Makena to see how well-endowed he was, and she'd been right. He was perfectly sculpted. Another *wow* flitted inside her head as she continued checking him out.

"Come on," Ben said, gripping her hand and tugging her toward the huge bed. She climbed in and laid on her side, watching as he opened the top drawer of his nightstand. He pulled out a foil packet and set it on top before dimming the lights with a small remote. It was dark enough to set a romantic mood, but not too dark where they couldn't see each other.

Ben climbed onto the bed next to her and propped up on one of his elbows. His gaze traveled the length of her body and he smiled as he stared down at her. The love brimming in his eyes made Makena all warm and tingly inside.

He's mine.

I'm his.

"Beautiful," he mumbled. "Absolutely beautiful."

"Funny, I was thinking the same thing," she cracked, throwing his words back at him.

Unable to stop herself, Makena ran her hand along Ben's body, over his chest, and past his flat abs. Her hand moved lower and she wrapped her fingers around his long, thick shaft, marveling at the weight of him. Leaning forward, she captured his mouth, kissing him with a hunger that she felt deep in her core, all the while gliding her hand up and down his length.

Ben groaned, the sound coming from somewhere deep within his chest. With his eyes closed, he moved against her hand as she continued to stroke him, slowly picking up the pace and increasing the pressure.

"That feels so good, but…" He inhaled suddenly and quickly covered her hand with his, stopping her mid-stroke. "Uhh…I, um…" he shook his head and moved her hand. "I don't want this over before we get started."

Makena wanted their time together to last as long as possible, too, but anxiousness spurred her on. She nudged Ben's shoulder, encouraging him onto his back, and amusement glittered in his eyes when she straddled him.

"I love the idea of you being on top," he said, his hands gripping her hips.

She didn't bother saying anything. Instead, her lips covered his and she kissed him with everything in her, hoping he could feel how much she loved him.

Ben groaned into her mouth, the sound vibrating into

her. One of his hands slid to her back and he flattened her against his hard body.

Mouth to mouth. Chest to chest. He gripped her hips as they ground against each other in a seductive rhythm. Her fog-filled brain could barely think straight with the way they were moving. The friction between her thighs grew more intense, stirring a desire within Makena that she hadn't felt in ages. All it would take was for her to move down a little, and he'd be inside of her, but like him, she didn't want to rush their time together.

*

Ben tightened his hold on Makena's hips as she moved on top of him. He wasn't even inside of her yet, and already he was on the edge of losing control. Having her body rubbed up against him was a dream come true. But if they kept going the way they were, he would lose it way before he wanted to.

"I want you so bad," he said gruffly, panting as if he had just done a hundred-yard sprint. "I want you now." He turned his body and flipped her onto her back, putting him on top.

Makena's startled gasp filled the room, and her eyes rounded.

He gave a slight shrug. "What? I can't wait any longer."

Makena burst out laughing, and Ben's heart swelled. He loved her laugh. Heck, he loved everything about the woman. From her sense of humor to her caring nature, she was everything he wanted in a mate.

And she was his.

He reached over and snatched the foil packet from the nightstand and ripped it open.

"Need some help?" Makena asked as he sheathed himself, a grin covering her sweet lips.

"Baby, if you help me, I'm going to explode." He brushed his lips across hers. "You can help me next time."

He kissed his way down from her mouth to her gorgeous full breasts and feasted on them. *Damn, she smells good,* he thought as his tongue swirled around her perky nipple. The erotic sounds she was making, and the way her body wiggled beneath him turned him on more. Before the night was over, he planned to taste every inch of her sexy body. But right now, he wanted to be buried deep inside of his woman.

He moved back up to her mouth and greedily devoured her sweetness while nudging her legs farther apart. When his erection brushed against Makena's sex, her sensual moan urged him on and he slowly entered her sweet heat.

She was so tight. Ben started moving, but stopped, afraid he'd hurt her before giving her body a chance to adjust to him.

"Don't. Don't you dare stop," she breathed, gripping his hips and pulling him in further.

Ben cursed under his breath and gritted his teeth. The sensation of being buried inside of her was almost too much.

His control was slipping.

She was right.

He couldn't stop.

Bracing one hand on the pillow next to her head, he slid his other hand down her side to the swell of her hip. Lifting slightly, Ben pushed in further. He wanted more than anything for their first time to be perfect...and to last, but she felt too good. At first his moves were slow, but he quickly picked up speed, going harder and deeper.

"Oh...yes," Makena panted.

The grip she had on his hips tightened as her nails dug into his skin. Ben didn't care. All he cared about was bringing her as much pleasure as she was bringing him.

With each thrust, she matched him stroke for stroke. Their moans mingled, and their breaths grew faster and louder as their tempo increased.

"Ahh...Ma...kena," Ben ground out, driving in and out of her like a man possessed, struggling against the intense sensation churned inside of him. He couldn't hold on. He... "Baby, I..."

"Ben!" Makena screamed her release. Her body

convulsed beneath him, and her head thrashed back and forth on the pillow. Her nails dug into his skin as the turbulence of her passion swirled around him.

Ben had never seen a more beautiful sight than her falling apart beneath him. Watching her sent him careening over the edge and he succumbed to the powerful orgasm that ripped through his body.

Collapsing on top of her, he quickly rolled onto his back as he gasped for air. "Woman...you damn near killed me," he said on a shuddering breath, and pulled her close.

Makena placed her hand on her heaving chest. "That was...that was intense," she said on a shaky laugh. "But, man...it was also amazing."

Ben couldn't agree more.

He also couldn't wait for round two.

Chapter Seven

The next morning, Makena slowly opened her eyes and squinted against the sliver of sunlight peeking through the blinds and hitting her dead in the face. She turned...or at least she tried to. Ben's hard body was hugged up behind her, and his heavy arm across her waist held her hostage.

A smile slid across her mouth as snippets of the night before invaded her brain. She and Ben have always had an emotional and mental connection. But last night their physical connection was stronger than anything Makena had ever experienced. She knew sharing her body with him would be amazing, but their lovemaking had exceeded her expectations.

But would things be awkward between them now? She had just slept—well, more than slept—with her best friend. Would she look at him any different? Would he have any regrets? She sure didn't, but what if...

"It's too early to be up." Ben's voice was deep and raspy close to her ear. He snuggled even closer, if that was possible. "Go back to sleep," he mumbled.

Makena could feel his hard body rubbed up against her backside. She wiggled her hips and smiled when he groaned.

"Keep that up, and you're going to get something started," he said, his hand doing a slow glide up to her breasts. He cupped one ever so gently. Caressing. Kneading.

Squeezing. Makena trembled and her eyes drifted shut when he tweaked her nipple and sent a zing of awareness shooting through her body. She wanted more than anything to pick up where they'd left off the night before, but she was wiped out. After two rounds of incredible lovemaking, her energy level was zilch.

"I thought you said that it was too early to be up," she said on a moan, covering his hand that had worked its way between her thighs.

"I did say that, didn't I?" He kissed that sensitive area behind her ear. "I love touching you…and holding you…and loving on you," he said between kisses. "I also love having you in my bed."

Makena moved to turn, forcing him to lift his arm, and she faced him. "I can't think of any other place I'd rather be."

She draped her arm across his waist, and her leg across him. They stared at each other and Makena wondered if the grin spreading across her face was as goofy as the one he was wearing.

It felt a little weird being in his bed naked, but not as strange as she thought it would be.

"Good morning," he said, still staring at her as if trying to memorize every aspect of her face.

Makena's heart squeezed at the love she saw glimmering in his eyes. "Good morning."

Ben leaned down and slowly kissed her. He nibbled on her lower lip, then her upper one before his tongue slid into the depths of her mouth. This was how she wanted to wake up every morning. Kissing, hugging, being loved on by the one man who made her feel alive.

As he deepened the kiss, an electric current charged through Makena's body sending a wave of desire pulsing through her veins.

Would she ever get enough of this man?

Never, the small voice in her head screamed. Their intense bond stirred so many emotions within Makena. She never wanted to come down off the high she was currently on. This new aspect of her and Ben's relationship was going to add something to her life that she'd been missing. Fun. Excitement. And an endless love that she'd been craving for years.

"I had fun with you last night," Ben murmured when the kiss ended.

"Yeah, me too. I thought it was going to be weird waking up next to you this morning."

His left brow inched up. "And what do you think now?"

She gave a small shrug. "No weirder than it was hearing you snoring like someone revving up a motorcycle." Makena's lips twitched, struggling to keep from grinning at the way his eyes narrowed.

"I see you got jokes. 'Cause I don't snore."

He poked her in the side, then tickled her until she erupted in a fit of giggles. When she got silly with Ben, it was easy to forget how old they were.

"That's all right, funny lady. Joke all you want. That's why I'm telling all of my friends I've seen you naked."

Makena's eyes rounded, and she punched him in the arm. "What are you, *twelve*?"

Ben's full-hearted laughter filled the quietness of the bedroom, and she slugged him again. That only made him laugh harder. "If you tell anybody what you saw last night or everything we did, I'm gonna—"

"What?" Still chuckling, he threw the covers off of them and climbed on top of her. "What'cha gon' do? Love on me the way you did last night?"

He nuzzled her neck and his large hand moved to one of her breasts. With an expert touch, he teased and tweaked a taut nipple, and jolts of pleasure pulsed through her veins.

"Tell me," he taunted. "What'chu gon' do?"

"I—I—I," Makena sputtered, arching into him as he kissed and licked his way down her body. With each stroke of his tongue on her heated skin, an explosion of tingles scurried through her. "I don't know," she finally said. "But…but I'll think of something."

Makena moaned the last words when his hand slid between her thighs.

Yeah, she'd think of something.

Later.

Much…much later.

*

Hours later, Makena put the last breakfast dish into the dishwasher. After another intense round of lovemaking, she and Ben had showered together, then prepared a hearty breakfast.

He had been right. So far, this new chapter in their relationship hadn't changed anything, except their physical relationship. They were still the same people who cherished each other's company.

"Are you sure you won't be able to make it to Sunday brunch?" Ben asked as he pulled the trash bag out of the garbage can. "I want the fam to know that we're officially dating now."

"I want them to know, too, but I can't make it this week."

Sunday brunch at the Jenkins estate was always entertaining; it was a bit like celebrating Christmas every week. Katherine Jenkins had started the tradition years ago, wanting her family to come together weekly to eat, drink, and hang out with each other. The estate was huge and easily accommodated the Jenkins clan.

But, as with family, there was always a lot of trash-talking, big reveals, and the occasional fight. There was never a dull moment, and Makena hated she was going to miss this Sunday.

"All right, then next week we'll tell everyone. I'm going to take this trash out. Be right back." He gave her a quick kiss on the lips.

They couldn't get enough of each other, both finding every reason to kiss and touch the other.

"I'll be ready to leave in ten," he said on his way out the back door.

"Sounds good."

Makena had plans to spend the afternoon with Ava and one of her friends from school. The fact her daughter still enjoyed spending time with her almost made Makena giddy. As long as she didn't start "acting weird," as Ava would say.

So what if Makena tried to show them that she was hip and could do the latest dances. And what was the big deal if she wanted to hug and kiss on her daughter in front of friends? How was that "acting weird"?

Today Makena planned to be cool and follow Ava's lead. Shopping with them was a safe enough activity that may not have either of the kids *accidentally* leaving her in a store.

Makena smiled at that thought and headed down the hallway to Ben's bedroom. She entered and walked straight to her overnight bag and purse that were sitting at the foot of the bed.

Heat rushed to her cheeks as she recalled all the delicious things she and Ben had done between the sheets. The man was insatiable, and she wouldn't have it any other way.

Makena's phone rang, and she hoped it wasn't her daughter calling to cancel. She dug the device from the side pocket of her purse and glanced at the screen. She didn't recognize the number, but answered anyway.

"Hello?"

"Attorney Nichols?"

"Yes, this is she."

"Hi, this is Gayle Holmes, Edward Foxall's caregiver. He gave me your contact information."

Unease crept through Makena. Had something happened to him? God, she hoped not. Not before she could arrange a meeting with him and Ben.

"Hi, Gayle. What can I do for you?"

"Edward passed away early this morning," she said quietly.

Makena's heart jolted. "Oh no. What happened?"

She closed her eyes and pinched the bridge of her nose as Gayle explained that Edward had caught pneumonia a few days ago. Makena tried focusing as the woman talked about bacteria spreading into his blood and causing complications, but her heart ached. Now there was no chance she could get Edward and Ben together. He would never know…

Hearing a sound at the bedroom door, her eyes flew open and her gaze collided with Ben. The concern on his face almost brought tears to Makena's eyes. How in the world was she going to share her suspicions with him?

"He died at seven o'clock this morning," Gayle was saying.

No longer able to look at Ben, Makena lowered her eyes and stared down at her navy-blue ballet flats. "Gayle, thank you for letting me know. And…I'm sorry for your loss. I saw the wonderful care you gave him. If there's anything you need, please let me know."

When Makena ended the call, Ben moved further into the room. He didn't speak until she looked up at him.

He reached for her hand. "What happened? Who is Edward?"

An acute sense of guilt stabbed her chest. Ben held a special spot in her heart, and they had always been honest with each other. What if her not sharing her suspicions earlier about Edward came back to haunt her? What if they were somehow related, and she hadn't said anything?

Then again, she could be making herself crazy for no reason. Edward insisted that he and Ben had never met. Maybe there had been no reason for them to meet. She could just be over-thinking the whole situation.

"Who was he to you, Makena?" Ben asked, his voice was more commanding, but held a bit of concern.

"He's a client. Or at least he was." She didn't want to discuss Edward, at least not yet. She grabbed her overnight bag and purse and started for the door. "He passed away a few hours ago."

Ben reached out and gently grabbed her arm, keeping her from walking away. "I'm sorry to hear that, but what else?"

Makena's brows furrowed. "What do you mean, what

else?"

"I mean, this is not the first time you've lost a client. Why are you so upset?"

"I'm not. I…" She shook her head and stuffed the phone back into her purse. "I just saw him a couple of weeks ago. I guess I'm…I'm shocked. I thought I had more time to…"

Crap. She didn't mean to say that. "We need to go. Ava is probably…"

Ben's cell phone vibrated on the nightstand, and he cursed under his breath. "You thought you had more time to what?" he said, ignoring the call.

"Get the phone. It might be important."

"Nothing is more important then you." He stood directly in front of her and lifted her chin with the pad of his finger, forcing her to make eye contact. "Quit stalling and tell me what's wrong. Who was this guy?"

"He's…it's nothing, really. Don't mind me. I'm just being overly emotional. He was in his late eighties, but his death was so sudden. I didn't know him well, but I liked him instantly."

"Why do I have a feeling there's still more you're not telling me?"

"Ben," she ground out in frustration, suddenly hating that he knew her so well. "Can we just not talk about this right now? Actually, we better get going. You're supposed to meet with Nate, and Ava and her friend are probably already at the house waiting for me."

Again, she tried to leave the room, but he blocked her. Taking the bag and her purse out of her hands, he set the items in a nearby chair and pulled her into his arms. It was pointless to try and resist because no one hugged the way he did.

Makena released a contented sigh and wrapped her arms around his waist. Her head rested against his chest. He always did this whenever he thought something was bothering her, or when trying to pry information out of her.

Ben ran a soothing hand up and down her back. "You know you can discuss anything with me, right?"

"I know, and I will." Seconds ticked by, and Makena lifted her head and looked at him. "Just not right now. Besides, we need to get going."

Ben studied her for a long minute, then brushed the back of his fingers down her cheek. "Are you going to be okay?"

She gave him a small smile. "Ben, I'm fine. I'm just all up in my feelings right now. Don't worry, though."

"I will always worry about you," he mumbled and brushed a kiss across her lips.

He moved to the nightstand where his wallet and cell phone were. Grabbing both items, he stuffed them into his pants pocket. He lifted her bag and nodded for her to precede him out the door.

Neither said a word as they walked through the house, turning out lights along the way. They stopped at the door that led into the garage.

"Question," Ben said, his hand hovering over the alarm keypad as he glanced over his shoulder at her. "This Edward guy, is he the same man who you said reminded you of me?"

Stunned by his question, Makena stared at him. She had totally forgotten that she'd told him that. Of course, he would remember. The man didn't forget anything. No matter how she answered, he'd come up with another question, but she couldn't outright lie to him.

"Yes, he reminded me a lot of you. So much so, I wanted you to meet him."

Chapter Eight

"I have the changes drafted, but at the rate their legal council is going, this merger is not going to happen on schedule," Liberty said, cutting into Ben's thoughts.

The associate lawyer had become a great asset since joining the firm a couple of years ago. After marrying his nephew and then having twins soon after, Ben assumed Liberty would take at least a year off. She hadn't. She took off eight weeks after the boys were born, but outside of regular vacation days, she made herself available to the firm. Which was exactly what Ben needed today.

His lack of focus was causing more harm than good. Had it not been for one of his partners, who had gone to court with him that morning, Ben would've screwed up their case. He couldn't afford to let his personal life compromise his business life. Yet, that's exactly what was happening.

Ben prided himself on being the best at whatever he set out to do, but his concentration was shot. He couldn't stop thinking about Makena. His mind volleyed between worrying about her, and agonizing over their future as a couple. They would forever be friends, but their new relationship wasn't going to work if she kept secrets from him. Granted, he might be making a big deal over nothing, but she had shut him out the day before, and their conversation that night was stilted at best.

He closed his eyes and rubbed his forehead as conversation at the table went on without much input from him. He couldn't be totally present until he got Makena to open up to him. He hadn't been in a serious relationship since his marriage, but there was one thing he'd learned back then. Communication was paramount.

"The merger agreement expires in six weeks. So they still have a little time, but I have a feeling they're going to ask for an extension," Liberty said.

"Our client won't allow an extension," Arnold, a partner, chimed in.

Tired of the back and forth, Ben said, "Arnold, let the client know what's going on. If they want this deal to move forward, they'll okay the extension. Liberty, for the rest of the week, I need your attention on the Carter case."

Ben's phone vibrated. It was facedown on the table next to his tablet, but he didn't turn it over to look at the screen. Instead, he finished what he was saying.

"We go back to court in a few days. Make sure *all* of our witnesses get added to the witness list. I don't want any surprises this time."

She nodded. "I'm on it."

While Arnold gave a few more instructions to Liberty and another associate lawyer, Ben tipped his cell so he could read the screen.

His pulse amped up.

Makena.

It didn't matter how old he was, his heart still pounded double-time when he heard from the woman he loved. Seeing her name and that she had sent a text made him cautiously optimistic that she was ready to tell him what was bothering her.

He skimmed the message.

MN: Please call me. Important.

The words *please* and *important* never went well together. The excitement moments ago vanished and in its place was unease clawing through him at the cryptic message. Ben pushed his chair back and stood.

"Excuse me for a minute. I need to take care of something," he said as he left the conference room and headed to his office. He called Makena's cell phone on the way. It rang twice before she picked up.

"Hey, sweetheart. I got your text." He stepped into his office and closed the door. "Everything okay?"

"Hi there. Yeah, everything is fine…actually, no. I need to talk to you. Do you have time today to come by my office?"

"I'll make time, but what's wrong?" Worry gnawed at Ben as he stood behind his desk and stared out the large window that overlooked a snow-covered park. Various scenarios raced through his mind. "Did something happen?"

Or maybe he should've asked what else happened. She'd been acting strange since receiving that call Saturday afternoon.

After a slight hesitation, Makena said, "This is about my client who passed away. I need…I…I don't want to talk about it over the phone. Is there any way you can come by soon? It's important."

By the tone of her voice, he knew it was important. But why would she need to talk to him about one of her clients? Unless… Was she in some type of legal trouble?

"Gotta wrap up a meeting first, and then I'll be there," he promised.

Ben disconnected the call and sat at his desk to review his afternoon schedule. It was packed. The good thing was that everything could be rescheduled, but there would be a price to pay.

He didn't care. Makena needed him.

He picked up his office phone and buzzed his assistant.

"Yes, Mr. Jenkins?"

"Claire, I need you to reschedule my afternoon appointments."

He heard her typing. "What about the meeting with

Allen Jackson? He's been waiting for two weeks."

Ben cursed under his breath and pinched the bridge of his nose, hating to cancel that one. "Tell him that I had an emergency. If he raises a stink, see if you can work him in this evening. Maybe a dinner meeting here at the office."

"Okay, I can do that. If he goes for the dinner idea, do you want me to have dinner delivered?"

"Text me if he's able to meet this evening, and order from Kendrick's. Get my usual and see what Allen wants."

"Will do, and I'll take care of rescheduling your other appointments."

"Okay. Thanks."

Thirty minutes later, Ben strolled into the office building where Makena worked, carrying a bouquet of white calla lilies in a crystal vase. She loved fresh flowers, and now that she was his woman, he planned to make sure she received them on a regular basis. Not just on special occasions. Lucky for him, there was a florist next door to his law firm.

Ben pushed the button to take him to the eleventh floor. His mind continued to speculate why Makena needed to see him. Originally, he thought she might be in legal trouble, but if that had been the case, she would've showed up at his office.

So what was so important that she couldn't discuss it over the phone? And since when did she talk about her clients with him, especially at her office?

The elevator dinged and the doors slid open. He stepped off and went left. Like so many office buildings these days, glass walls encased the individual suites. He passed by a couple where only their waiting rooms and receptionists could be seen.

Ben slowed when he reached the offices of Holmes, Baker & Nichols. The firm was smaller than his and only dealt with estate planning and family law. He had wanted Makena to join Jenkins & Associates after she moved back to town, but she had shot down that idea. Now, Ben was glad she had. There was no way he'd get any work done working in close quarters with her. Yet, he still wouldn't mind her joining his team.

He pushed open the glass door that led into their office suite. The receptionist, a young woman who had been with the firm almost a year, glanced up. She greeted him with a smile and lifted her finger, requesting that he give her a minute.

Ben nodded and stepped away from the counter. Instead of waiting for the receptionist to finish her call, he texted Makena. Seconds later, she appeared and warmth spread through his body. She didn't wear bright colors to work often, but the stunning red two-piece pantsuit brought out the warmth of her skin tone.

Makena smiled as they moved toward each other, but the smile didn't quite reach her eyes. Even the flowers didn't brighten her mood.

Ben didn't get anxious about much, but not knowing what was going on with her bugged the heck out of him.

"Those are beautiful," she whispered, accepting the flowers and stepping into his open arms. "You know you didn't have to buy me flowers."

"Yeah, actually I did since I'm planning to spoil you."

Finally, she gave him a genuine smile that lit up the room. "Thanks for coming by so quickly."

He gave her a quick peck on the lips. "Of course." He held onto her with one arm still around her waist not wanting to let her go. It had only been thirty-some hours since he'd last seen her, but it felt like a week.

"How was traffic?" she asked when he released her.

"Not too bad."

As they made their way down the hall, Ben kept his hand at the small of her back. The need to touch her was as strong as his need to breathe. He'd had it bad for Makena for so long; now that they were together, that need to be near her had intensified.

When they made it to her office, Ben closed the door. The moment she set the vase on a nearby book stand, he backed her up to the wall. It probably wasn't the time, but he had missed her. He needed to show her how much.

Lowering his head, his mouth covered hers. At first, she was hesitant, then her hands slid slowly up his chest and she wrapped her arms around his neck. As their tongues tangled, some of his anxiety seeped away. All that mattered at the moment was that they were together.

Ben deepened the kiss when Makena's hand went to the back of his head and she held him close. Their moans mingled; they were the only sounds in the office. If only they were somewhere a little more private. Ben wanted more than just her mouth. He wanted her entire body.

As if reading his mind, Makena stiffened in his arms and ripped her mouth from his. "Knock it off. I knew you would try and distract me."

He kept one arm round her waist and lifted her chin, forcing her to look at him.

"Then talk to me. What's going on?"

Makena released a noisy sigh and stepped out of his hold. "I called you here for business. There's something you need to know."

Ben put a little distance between them, forcing himself to keep his hands to himself. Makena didn't play games, and one of the things he loved most about her was that she was always forthcoming. Normally. This cold-and-hot behavior she'd been exhibiting over the weekend and right now was making him crazy.

Shoving his hands into the front pockets of his pants, he watched as she walked across her large office. She stopped next to the small round conference table in the corner and waved her hand toward the empty chair for him to sit.

Once they were seated, Makena opened a manila folder. "As you know, one of my clients recently passed." She paused and swallowed. "He named you in his will."

Ben's brows shot up as shock jockeyed inside his chest. "Say what?" he asked, trying to make sense of what Makena just said. "Who's your client? Wait." He shook his head as if that would clear the fog that suddenly consumed him. "Are you telling me that the *Edward* guy, the one who died the other day, the same one who reminded you of me, included me in his will?"

"More than included you. You're his only beneficiary," she rasped, then cleared her throat. "His name is...was Edward Foxall, and he set up his will to be payable immediately after his death."

Ben sat in a state of shock as he listened to her tell him he had inherited land that was north of the Mount Lookout area. Makena handed him several photos as she explained that the property was several acres and was a buildable lot with utilities.

"According to Edward, there are no liens on the property. He's owned it free and clear for over twenty years. He just never did anything with it."

Ben studied the pictures as the shock of what he was receiving settled inside of him. If it was the area that he was thinking of, the grassy, heavily-treed land was worth at least a half a million dollars. Financially, he was very comfortable, but adding the property to his portfolio would put him easily at millionaire status.

Ben shook his head again, struggling to understand why someone he didn't know would leave him land. "I don't know this guy. Why would he leave me anything—let alone a half a million-dollar property. Tell me about Edward."

Makena shrugged. "I don't know much. He came to the office a couple of weeks ago and said he wanted to hire me to make out his will."

Makena explained that the eighty-nine-year-old was very alert and charming, and had insisted on her calling him Edward. He had told her that he didn't have anything as far as assets, except the land.

"He was clear on how he wanted his will handled after his death. I'm starting to think that he knew he wasn't going to be around much longer. He had visible health issues, but his mind was sharp. He knew what he was doing and knew what he wanted."

Ben glanced at the photos again before returning his attention to Makena. "Of all the estate lawyers in the city, how did he find you? Did he know you knew me?"

Her brows drew together, and she tilted her head. "Good questions. I have no idea. I thought it was just by chance that I happened to know you, but..."

"What did you say when he mentioned me being his beneficiary?"

"Nothing. At first, I thought maybe it was another Benjamin Jenkins, but then he gave me your home address, and he knew things."

"Things like what?"

"He said he liked what you were doing to make Cincinnati better. He even knew about your involvement in the new community center and that you and Nate had a property development company. He said he couldn't think of a better person to leave the land to."

Ben propped his elbow on the table and ran his hand down his chin. Who the hell was the guy? If Ben had a non-profit or an organization that could benefit from the property, then he could understand the gift. He was co-owner of a property development company, not a grassroots charity.

"Are you sure you don't know him?" Makena asked, her tone almost pleading as she stared at him.

Ben quickly ran through his mental rolodex. He was good with names and faces, and Edward Foxall didn't ring a bell. "Sweetheart, I have no idea who he is. Do you have a photo of him?"

She shook her head. "I couldn't find one of him online. He wasn't on any social media platform. Not surprising, since he was nearly ninety."

Her shoulders sagged, and disappointment marred her beautiful face. When she stood and carried the file to her desk, Ben didn't stop her. He just watched.

Makena didn't sit in her office chair. Instead, she set the file down. Placing her hands, palms down on top of the desk, she lowered her head.

Why was she so torn up about this client?

"What aren't you telling me?" Ben asked, his tone rougher than intended.

Makena's head jerked up, and she glanced at him as if temporarily forgetting he was in the room. "Excuse me?"

"It's obvious that this case is bothering you. I want to know why. Sure, it's never easy losing anyone, but this guy was a client. A new client. What am I missing here, Makena? What's wrong?"

She folded her lower lip between her teeth and straightened. "I think... I mean, I'm not sure, but..." Her words trailed off and the weariness in her eyes earlier returned.

Ben studied her for a minute, noting how tense she was. She looked as if she hadn't slept in days. And if the way she rubbed the side of her forehead was any indication, she was also battling a headache. He had never seen her like this, and he wasn't leaving until he knew what the hell was going on.

He slowly rounded the desk and reached for her. "Come here." Relief flooded through him when she stepped into his embrace. She snuggled into him, her head resting in the crook of his neck, and Ben breathed her in. The vibrant, coconut scent of her hair always calmed him in a way he couldn't get anywhere else. He hoped that he was somehow giving her the same type of peace.

They stood that way in silence, wrapped in each other's arms for several minutes, before he spoke.

"I don't like seeing you like this, and you're starting to worry me. Talk to me," he said, placing a gentle kiss near her ear. "I want to know what it was about Edward that has you rattled. What are you holding back?"

Makena eventually lifted her head and looked at him. "I think...I think he might be your father."

Chapter Nine

"What?" Ben yelled, looking at Makena wide-eyed, as if she had lost her mind.

Maybe she had. The idea that Edward Foxall and he could be father and son was beyond far-fetched. Everyone always said how much Ben favored his dad, Steven Jenkins. But the resemblance between Ben and Edward was too startling to be a coincidence.

"Okay, maybe not your father."

"Damn straight he's not my father! Babe, what the hell?"

Makena held onto the front of his suit jacket to keep him from moving away from her. "Just hear me out. I can't explain it, but I think…I mean…I have a feeling…"

Frustration drummed through her. She was ruining this conversation. So many thoughts ran through her mind at once. She couldn't decide what to say and what to keep to herself. Most of what she was thinking was speculation. She didn't have any hard facts to support her theory. Except…

"So what if the guy and I favor each other?" Ben eased out of her hold. "Everyone has a twin in this world. Besides, you know practically my whole family. If we were related, you would've met him long before now."

"Ben, you didn't see him. You two had the same eyes, and there's no one in your family with your eyes. Even some of your facial expressions and mannerisms were the exact same as Edward's."

Makena needed Ben's natural curiosity to kick in. She didn't miss the way his eyes had lit up when he looked through the pictures of the land. He loved real estate almost as much as she loved shoes. She wanted him to dig for answers. For instance, who was Edward to him? Why'd he really leave the land? If Edward had known so much about Ben, then why hadn't he reached out to Ben?

The whole situation had Makena on edge as her inquisitive nature ran wild. Outside of the night she had spent with Ben, she hadn't been sleeping well. Guilt, though misplaced, continued to plague her for the past few weeks.

If only she'd been able to get the two men together before Edward passed. She believed with all her heart that there was something Edward hadn't told her. Something important. Something that had everything to do with Ben.

Makena couldn't shake the feeling that the two men were somehow related. But how? Ben was right. She knew most of the Jenkins clan and many of Katherine's side of the family, and Ben definitely favored his father. Yet, out of hundreds of relatives, no one had his light-brown, almost hazel eyes, except for his youngest son.

Ben rubbed the back of his neck as he paced in front of her desk. She could almost hear the wheels in his head churning as his shoes tapped against her wood floors. He knew her well enough to know she wouldn't just throw crazy ideas out like that.

The notion that there might be some family secret tied up with Edward wasn't far from her thoughts. But she didn't want to do anything to cause trouble. They were like family to her as well. Yet, if her suspicions were right, Ben had a right to know. Makena just hoped her suspicions and butting in didn't come back to bite her in the ass.

"I called Michael," she blurted

Ben stopped, and his head snapped to her with his mouth hanging open. "*Seriously?* You called a private investigator?"

Michael Cutter wasn't just an investigator. He was Peyton Jenkins' husband, Ben's niece who used to run Jenkins & Sons Construction before moving to New York. The former NYPD-detective-turned-private-investigator was the best in the field. Makena had never needed his services, but even though Michael lived in New York, Ben's law firm used him often.

She had probably overstepped, but Ben meant the world to her. He had a right to know exactly who Edward was to him.

"Mac, sweetheart, maybe Edward Foxall is a distant relative, but I've never heard of him. I don't understand why you're so—"

"It's a gut feeling," she interrupted, getting more agitated with each passing minute.

Deep in her soul, she knew there was something more to Edward leaving the land than just a kind gesture to a community leader. Ben knew it, too, even if he wasn't ready to speculate.

"I didn't give Michael any details. I just told him that we—and in we, I mean you—might need his help with something real soon." She shrugged. "Maybe Edward was being honest with his reasons for making you his only beneficiary, but what if he wasn't? What if there's something else that you should know about him or even the property?"

Makena didn't want to involve Ben's parents or siblings. She couldn't explain her reasoning, except the feeling of dread swimming in her gut.

"Aren't you curious?" she asked. "The guy comes out of nowhere and leaves you a plot of land. Not just any land. Prime real estate. Don't you want to know who he is and why he left it to you?"

Ben huffed out a breath and ran his hand over his head. "I'll admit, I'm curious. But that doesn't make me think that the man is my long-lost Pops." He paused. "So maybe I'll see if they've heard—"

"No. Call Michael."

Ben stood frozen on the other side of the desk, studying her. "Surely you weren't serious when you suggested this guy might be my father," he said carefully as he moved toward her. "Because that's impossible. I know who my parents are. There's no way in hell this guy could be who you think he is."

"But what if—"

"No." Ben shook his head. "What's gotten into you? I've never known you to act irrational."

"Am I acting irrational? I know this isn't the news you expected, but we need to find out the truth. When it comes to you, there's *nothing* I wouldn't do." Even if it meant angering people who she respected, she'd do that for Ben to know the truth. Whatever that truth might be.

"You honestly think there's some deep, dark secret that Edward Foxall is at the center of?" Ben's words were spoken low with a hint of disbelief behind each one. "If that's what's going on in that beautiful mind of yours, forget about it. There are no secrets in the Jenkins family. No secret babies. Hell, most of the family can't keep a secret to save their life. What you're suggesting is crazy."

Makena swallowed the lump in her throat. She absolutely adored the Jenkins family. But if there was something they hadn't told Ben... If by chance he and Edward were really related, he needed to know.

She lifted her chin and stared him in those beautiful eyes that she loved so much. "Call and give Michael the go-ahead. Or I will."

*

The intercom on Ben's desk buzzed, and he pounded his fist on the small pile of file folders. "I said no interruptions," he snapped at Claire, his assistant, something he'd been doing for the last two days.

Yeah, Ben knew he was being a jerk, but waiting to hear something from Mike was wearing on his nerves.

"I'm sorry, sir, but your brother Thomas is here. He's insisting on seeing you."

"Tell him I'm busy." It wasn't a total lie. Ben had a

couple of legal briefs on his desk that needed his attention. The last thing he wanted was for Thomas to barge in, asking for a favor. The man never stopped by the firm unless he wanted Ben to do something for him.

There was a quick knock before his office door swung open. Thomas strode in with Claire running behind him.

Ben tossed his pen on the desk and slammed back in his chair. "What part of *I'm busy* don't you understand?" he barked, and glared at his oldest brother, who didn't seem the least bit phased by Ben's outburst.

"Mr. Jenkins, I'm so sorry. I told him—"

"It's all right, Claire. He has the habit of acting like he owns every place he walks into."

Thomas removed the black fedora from his head and unbuttoned his suit jacket. He rarely wore an overcoat, even in thirty-degree weather. Instead, he was decked out in a navy-blue three-piece wool suit, looking every bit the CEO of a manufacturing company.

He and Ben were around the same height, shared the same skin color, and had a similar style of dress. But where Ben enjoyed chilling in a T-shirt and jeans, his brother was a little stuffier and rarely dressed down.

Thomas dropped into one of the guest chairs in front of Ben's desk. "Sorry, but I needed to talk to you. Since you've been ignoring my calls, little brother, I had to stop by."

Claire backed out of the office without another word, closing the door behind her. She'd been with Ben for over ten years. This wasn't her first dealings with one of his pushy family members.

Ben rubbed his forehead, trying to tap down his frustration. "What's so important that you had to interrupt me when I'm trying to get some work done?"

Thomas folded his arms across his wide chest. "What's your problem? I can understand you having a funky attitude with me, but not to Claire. I heard the way you snapped at her when she told you I was here."

Yeah, he needed to apologize to her later. Ben didn't

make it a habit of being hard to work with. Yet, she'd been dealing with his jacked-up attitude for days now and not once had she complained.

"So what's up?" Thomas prompted. "What's got you in a bad mood? A tough case?"

"It's nothing," Ben bit out.

After leaving Makena's office the other day, he thought about calling his brother. Ben wanted to question Thomas and see if he knew of Edward Foxall or had heard the name before, but decided not to. He hoped more than anything that Makena was off base in her assumptions, but he knew better. She wouldn't have pushed so hard if she didn't think something was up with Edward.

"What do you want, Thomas? I have work to do."

"Dang, man. You act like I only come by when I want something. Maybe I wanted to invite you to lunch."

"Do you?" Ben challenged.

"It depends."

"On?"

"On whether you help me with—"

"No," Ben said before giving him a chance to finish. He picked up his pen and went back to the brief he'd been trying to read before the interruption.

"Come on, man. It's not like I ask for much. I just need you to look over an expansion proposal for me."

Ben shook his head. "Thomas, your company retains legal counsel. Get them to look at it."

"I plan to, but I wanted your opinion before I present to our board of directors."

There was another knock on the door, and Ben huffed out a breath. This time he caught himself before growling *come in.* "Yes?" he said, and the door eased open.

"You wanted to see me?" Luke Hayden asked before noticing his father-in-law sitting near the desk. "Hey, what's up, Dad? I didn't know you were here."

The two men exchanged a handshake and a one-armed hug.

"Hey, son," Thomas said. Luke was married to Thomas' youngest daughter, Christina, or CJ, as the family called her.

Thinking about the chance that he wasn't really a Jenkins had Ben's pulse spinning cartwheels. He'd been keeping a low profile for the last couple of days, not in the mood to talk to or be around anyone, not even Makena.

What if she was right? What if he was somehow related to Edward?

I think he might be your father, Makena's words played through his mind.

The idea was ludicrous, but Ben knew that nothing was outside the realm of possibility—even deep dark family secrets meant to stay buried. But Makena had brought up the one thing that had Ben second-guessing everything he knew about his life.

His eye color.

Growing up, he wondered why he was the only one who didn't have dark brown eyes. When he'd asked his parents, they claimed genetics, saying that maybe one of my great-great-great grandparents had the unusual eye color.

As the years passed, it hadn't mattered. Ben was a Jenkins. He looked like them. He acted like them. He even sounded like many of them.

He has your eyes, Makena had said.

Part of him was upset that she insisted on digging into Edward's life. The other part of him was reminded of why he loved her so much. She was only looking out for his best interest like usual. He just wasn't sure he was ready for whatever Mike dug up.

"Good, I'd appreciate it," Thomas said, cutting into Ben's thoughts. Ben had missed most of their conversation, but it sounded like he was off the hook. Maybe Luke had agreed to do whatever it was Thomas wanted done.

"Ben is acting like a jerk. Like he's too busy to do me this one solid."

"Whatever, Thomas. Luke, you just make sure you don't do his bidding on company's time."

Luke had been a well-sought-after defense attorney in New York before moving to Cincinnati. Ben's other niece, Martina, had dubbed him the *Thug Lawyer,* claiming he had serious swagger and was a little gangster-like. Ben had to admit that Luke was a beast in the courtroom. Since being with Jenkins & Associates, he hadn't lost a case yet.

"Okay, I gotta get out of here," Thomas said, buttoning his jacket and slipping his hat back on. "Ben, whatever's got your shorts in a knot, fix it and quit acting like a knucklehead."

"Man, just go," Ben said to his brother's retreating back.

"You wanted to see me?" Luke asked, leaning on the back of one of the chairs.

"How do you feel about being second-chair on the Carter's case?'

Luke shrugged. "I'm cool with that. What about Jon?"

"He'll still be on the team. He's actually the one who suggested pulling you in on the case. He's thinking your defense background will—"

"Excuse me, Mr. Jenkins."

Ben glanced around Luke to see Claire standing in the doorway with a large envelope.

"Yes?"

"The package you've been expecting just arrived."

Ben's stomach tightened as she moved further into the office with a thick, padded envelope. She held it out to him, and he stared at it for a long minute before accepting it.

He must've hesitated a minute too long if the curious expression on Luke's face was any indication.

"Thanks, Claire."

"You all right?" Luke asked the moment Claire left the office and closed the door behind her. "You've been acting strange for a couple of days now. Folks around here are afraid to ask you anything. And now you're staring at that envelope as if you're expecting it to grow legs and run out of here."

Ben grunted and shook his head at the visual Luke's

words evoked.

"So what's going on?" he asked, straightening to his six foot height, and crossing his thick arms across his chest. The move made him look intimidating.

Unlike all the other men in the office, Luke didn't have on a tie. Today, he was dressed in a charcoal gray suit and a turtleneck that was a shade lighter. Trendy, yet professional, the kid was definitely a guy who marched to his own beat.

Ben held the FedEx package with both hands as his eyes skimmed over Mike's New York address. "It's a personal matter," he finally said. Even though he trusted Luke with his life, this was something Ben was keeping quiet until he got answers.

"Okay. Well, you know where to find me if you need me. In the meantime, I'll touch basis with Jon."

"Thanks. I appreciate that."

After Luke left him alone, Ben continued to stare at the large envelope. Dread seeped into his body and tunneled to the depths of his soul. He already knew he wasn't going to like what he was about to learn.

Dropping the packet onto the desk, he stood and walked over to the office door, locking it. When he returned to his desk, he ripped open the package. A note was on the top of the pile.

Brace yourself, and call me if you need anything else. FYI, I haven't said a word to anyone, and I won't. Mike.

Ben's jaw tightened, and the sudden lump in his throat plunged to the pit of his stomach with a thud. With that cryptic note, what the hell was he about to learn?

Instead of prolonging the inevitable, he dived into the packet of material. On top of the pile was a photo, and Ben's heart slammed against his chest. The picture was a close-up of a man in an army jacket and helmet, who looked like he could have been Ben thirty years ago. But it was the man's light eyes that caused a chill to scurry over Ben's skin.

Eyes that were identical to his.

Heart racing, Ben dropped the picture as if it was on fire

and bolted out of his chair. Who the hell was Edward Foxall to him? Because there was no denying that they were related. But how?

Suddenly unable to breathe, he tugged on the knot of his tie. He yanked it back and forth to loosen what felt like a noose around his neck. There had to be an explanation for this. It was no wonder Makena had struggled to tell him about Edward. The guy could be his...

No. Don't even go there.

There was no way this guy could be anyone to him, Ben told himself, but deep down he knew there was no denying it. Not only was he probably related, he was closely related.

He dropped back down in his seat. Adrenaline pumped through his veins as he frantically went through the documents like a man possessed.

Birth certificate.

Military ID.

Photos.

Ben skimmed every piece of paper looking for anything that would tie him to the man. He kept sifting through the pile of information until he stumbled upon another birth certificate.

His heartbeat sped up, pounding hard enough for people down the hall to hear. He quickly scanned the certificate in search of a name...his.

Instead, it read: *Cheryl Foxall.* Date of birth: *January 16, 1948.* Mother's name: *Edna Langly.* Father's name: *Edward Foxall.*

If he has a daughter, why leave the land to me?

The question was still rattling in his head when he found another photo. It was of Edward and a little girl, a preteen, standing awkwardly next to each other on a beach. There were a few other pictures of them, and one thing was clear. If the girl in the photo was his daughter, they weren't very close. They both looked as if they'd rather be anywhere else but together.

He then found two death certificates. *Edna Langly.* Date

of death: *November 3, 1970. Cheryl Foxall.* Date of death: *February 28, 1990.*

Ben would've been three years old when Edna died and twenty-three when Cheryl died.

Head spinning and eyes burning, he propped his elbows on his desk and covered his face with his hands. What did all of this mean? Who were these people?

One question after another bombarded his mind. It was as if he was on a rollercoaster going downhill at a hundred miles an hour without brakes. He had to talk to his parents, but right now that was the last thing he wanted to do.

Because deep down, he knew he wasn't going to like the answers.

His cell phone, sitting on the edge of his desk, rang. Ben glanced at the device.

Makena.

He hadn't talked to her all day, and he wasn't sure if he could speak without getting emotional. As it was, he could barely breathe.

The phone stopped ringing, but a second later, it started again. Seeing that it was Makena calling back, he answered.

"I received some information," he mumbled, the quiver in his voice matched the rapid beat of his heart. "You were right about…" he started, but stopped when the pressure of emotion built inside his chest.

"Oh, baby…where are you?" Makena asked in a rush. "Mike called and said you might need me. Are you at the office?"

Ben couldn't speak. All he could do was stare at the pictures of Edward and the woman. He feared his life was about to change and there wasn't a damn thing he could do about it.

"I'm on my way," Makena said.

Still, Ben couldn't speak.

Chapter Ten

Makena was at a loss. She stood in the opening between her dining room and living room, unsure of what to do about Ben. He hadn't said ten words since she'd picked him up from work, and she was starting to worry.

After calling him earlier and hearing the pain in his voice, she knew he had gone through the information that Mike had put together. She had no idea what was sent, but for Mike to call her, asking that she check on Ben, meant it had to be serious. And then to call Ben and hear the strangled emotion in his voice, she couldn't get to him fast enough.

Now, looking at him stare at the television bothered her. There was a basketball game on the screen, but the TV was muted. Ben didn't seem to be paying much attention. He hadn't spoken, hadn't moved, just sat there. Even when she suggested they go through the packet Mike had sent together, he shot down the idea, saying he'd seen enough.

Releasing a frustrated breath, Makena headed back to the dining room table where she had Edwards information spread out. She picked up his army picture and shook her head. There was no denying it. He and Ben were related. If she thought they resembled each other when Edward had visited her office, that was nothing compared to the photo. A younger Edward and Ben could've been twins back in the day. The genes were too strong to deny.

What Makena hadn't found, though, was anything that clearly linked the two men. As she stuffed the items back into the envelope, she scrutinized everything. There was nothing in the information that named Ben as a relative, friend, or anything else.

"I'm gonna get going."

Makena's head jerked up. Ben stood several feet away, as if afraid to get close to the information spread out on the table. He definitely wasn't himself. The five-o'clock shadow covering his cheeks and chin gave him a sexy, rugged appearance, but it wasn't him.

Normally clean-shaven and immaculately dressed on a workday, his suit was wrinkled, his eyes were red, and he looked exhausted.

"Where are you going?" She walked over to him and slid her arms around his waist. He hugged her back, but it wasn't one of his usual soul-stirring hugs. "I thought you were staying the night."

"Not tonight," he said with no emotion.

Makena couldn't ever remember a time when he was this somber. He was always upbeat. Occasionally, he might be distracted by a case or something else, but nothing like this and never with her. Who could blame him, though? She had a ton of questions about Edward and Cheryl and how they fit into Ben's life. No doubt he had twice as many questions.

"Tell me what you're thinking," she said, needing him to give her more than two-worded answers.

"I'm thinking it's been a long day."

"All the more reason why you should stay here, relax, and let me cook you some dinner."

Finally, his arms tightened around her and he pulled her closer, burying his face in the crook of her neck. Yet, he didn't respond to the dinner offer.

Makena's heart broke for him. She felt his pain. He wasn't one to show emotion, but this new development in his life clearly had shaken him. But what worried her more was that he still didn't know who Edward was.

Ben told her that he planned to talk to his parents. He just hadn't decided when. Right now, he didn't want to talk to anyone. Not her, and especially not anyone in his family.

But what would happen when he got all the answers?

"Don't go," Makena said quietly. The last thing he needed was to be alone. "Stay with me," she added.

They'd been at her house for hours. In addition to being tired, he had to be hungry. Each time she offered him something to eat, he declined, saying he wasn't hungry.

"I can't. Not tonight." He placed a lingering kiss on Makena's cheek before releasing her.

"Are you mad at me?" she blurted out.

It was her fault that his life might've just changed forever and not in a good way. If her suspicions were right—and she was ninety-nine percent sure they were—his parents had some explaining to do. There were some deep, dark secrets in the Jenkins family, and they would soon come out.

And it's all my fault, she thought.

If she hadn't pushed and insisted, Ben might not have looked into Edward. Then again, maybe he would have. It wasn't every day someone you've never heard of leaves you land valued at a half-million dollars.

"Of course, I'm not mad at you," he finally said. "I just…I just need time to process what little I know about this situation, and prepare myself for all that I don't know."

Makena nodded, finding little comfort in knowing he didn't blame her for possibly turning his world upside down.

"All right, then I'll drive you home." They had left his car at the office, not even thinking about how or when he'd go back and get it.

Makena started for the stairs, but Ben stopped her.

"I don't want you out driving this late at night. I called for an Uber. It should be here shortly."

"Then I guess I'm riding with you, because I don't want—"

"Sweetheart," Ben cupped her cheek, "I'll be fine. I'm

going home to get some sleep, then I might go by my parents' house sometime tomorrow."

"Do you want me to go with you?"

He dropped his hand and shook his head. "Nah, this is something I need to do myself. All I ask is that you not say anything to anyone, yet, especially my fam…" His voice trailed off, and he ran his hand over his head, letting it slide to the back of his neck, and sighed.

"Babe, no matter what you find out or what happens with your parents, they will always be your family," Makena said with authority. She got in his face, needing him to hear her. "I don't know how Edward fits into your life, but there's no doubt that you're a Jenkins and always will be."

He nodded and looked away. Stuffing a hand in the front pocket of his suit pants, he pulled out his cell phone.

"My ride is here."

"Ben, please…either cancel the ride or let me go home with you."

"Mac, I'm cool. I'll text you when I get home." He grabbed the envelope from the table, kissed her, and then left her staring after him.

God only knew what he'd find out tomorrow. She just hoped it wasn't anything that would destroy the strong relationship he had with his family.

Only time will tell.

Chapter Eleven

Two days later, Ben pulled onto his parents' massive estate and drove up the long, double-wide driveway. He parked on the side of the house behind his brother Thomas' car. It was almost nine o'clock at night, and he had hoped that his parents were home alone. He shouldn't be surprised, though. They were night owls, and it wasn't unusual for someone in the family to be there at all hours of the day.

He released a noisy sigh and laid back against the headrest without turning off the car. The headache that had been brewing inside his skull for the last couple of days intensified. He could always leave and return another day, but that would just be prolonging the inevitable.

"I should've called," he mumbled. He had actually tried, but each time he picked up the phone to dial his father, Ben changed his mind.

He would never be ready to talk to his parents about Edward. He had no hard facts that proved he was related to the guy, except for the photos. Yet, deep in his heart, he knew there was a connection. A strong connection. A connection that was still a mystery to him.

Makena might not have been serious when she said that Edward might be his father, but anything was possible. And if that was the case, it would mean his mother...

Ben couldn't even finish the thought. Katherine Jenkins would never step out on her husband. Ben would bet his life on that.

He was missing something, and there was only one way to find out what.

He climbed out of his SUV, went around to the back of the house, and let himself in. A burst of laughter erupted and it was clear that Thomas wasn't the only one there.

Ben trudged through the long hallway that led to the front of the house, feeling as if he carried a boulder on his back. There wasn't much that made him nervous, but this situation had his stomach churning with anxiety. He hadn't even talked to his parents yet and already he felt like he was going to throw up.

It's now or never, he thought and stopped in the kitchen doorway. His mother was slicing up cake and his father was leaning against the breakfast bar, talking to those at the table.

Ben's brother Thomas and his wife Violet, along with Carolyn and her husband Lincoln, were camped out at the table with dessert plates in front of them. They were dressed up as if just returning from the theater or some other event.

Had he'd known all of them would be there, he would've postponed his visit…again.

"Hey, son," his mother greeted, her smile as inviting as usual. She met him halfway and wrapped her arms around him. "I didn't know you were stopping by. Are you hungry?"

Ben gave a head nod and a lazy wave to those at the table. "No, I'm good, but I need to talk to you and Pops…alone."

The thick silence that suddenly filled the space was new. That never happened in a Jenkins household. The family as a whole was just loud, even when they weren't trying to be.

His father pushed away from the counter and clamped his large hand on Ben's shoulder and gave it a little squeeze. That was typically how he greeted his boys, or he'd clapped them on the back, then draped his arm around their shoulders. "We can talk in my office," he said.

Even in his eighties, Steven Jenkins—lovingly known as Pops or Grampa—was a force. His powerful presence often made people wither beneath his stare.

At over six feet tall with a broad chest and wide shoulders, he looked like a former football player. The few wrinkles in his face and the slight beer belly did nothing to detract from his good looks. The old saying *black don't crack* fit him perfectly.

His father walked into the office first, turned on the lights and made a beeline to the bar in the corner of the room.

"Want a drink?" he asked, holding up a bottle of Crown Royal. His father wasn't a big drinker, but enjoyed a glass of whiskey on occasion.

"No, I'm good. Thanks," Ben murmured.

"What's going on?" Pops asked, just as Ben's mother strolled into the room, closing the door behind her.

They both sat on the sofa next to each other while Ben stood near the huge desk. Now that he had both of their attention, he wasn't sure where to start.

His mother's concerned gaze met his. "Are you okay? Did something happen?" she asked.

Ben sucked in a long breath, then released it slowly. "I'm all right, but something happened the other day. I'm hoping you guys can fill in some gaps for me."

His father's brows furrowed. "Something like what happened?"

"Someone named Edward Foxall recently died and left me a plot of land worth a half-million dollars."

"Oh, dear God," his mother gasped, her unsteady hand hovering over her mouth. Tears filled her eyes, but none fell as she glanced at Ben's father.

Ben wasn't sure if she was shocked, upset, or at a loss. He also couldn't tell if the *Oh, dear God* was for his benefit, because of something she knew, or if it was for Edward losing his life.

Steven Jenkins was as cool and calm as usual, a trait that

had served him well over the years during business dealings. Ben could count on one hand the number of times he'd seen his father rattled. Those few instances had to do with Ben's mother. Pops was intensely protective of her. If anyone made her cry or tried to hurt her in any way, he'd be out for blood.

"How'd he die?" his father asked.

That answered one question for Ben. They knew Edward.

"Complications from pneumonia. Care to tell me how you knew him?" Ben asked dryly, anger simmering beneath the surface as he stared his father in the eyes.

With his arm around his wife, Pops sipped his drink, never taking his gaze from Ben. "Question is, how did you know him?"

Ben hated games, and he felt as if he'd been tossed smack in the middle of one. He paced near the desk, trying to rein in the anger that was building and picking up speed.

These were his parents, he reminded himself. No matter what the conversation uncovered, that was something he was going to try and remember.

"I never met him. I never even heard of the guy until the other day," Ben said, still pacing. Anything to keep from looking at them. "Imagine my surprise when I found out I was his beneficiary. Not only that, I'm the splitting image of him." Ben turned to them, digging deep for that calm that served him well in the courtroom.

"Tell him," his mother said with authority. She was the only person who could get away with talking to his father in that no-nonsense tone.

Pops released a long drawn-out sigh and leaned forward. He propped his elbows on his knees, and his large hands were securely wrapped around his glass of whiskey.

"What do you already know?" he asked, without looking at Ben.

"Not much, which is why I'm here."

His father sipped his whiskey, taking his time before responding. "I had a cousin named Terrance Jenkins. He was actually a second cousin, who was about ten or twelve years younger than me."

Anxiousness drummed through Ben. He listened intently while his father described this cousin who he'd been fond of. It didn't go unnoticed to Ben that he spoke of him in the past tense. That only amped up his anxiety.

"Terrance was your biological father," Pops said quietly.

For Ben, the declaration was like a bomb blasting inside of his skull. He shook his head.

"Excuse me?" he heard himself say as he dropped down into a nearby chair.

Why was he surprised? For the last couple of days, he had prepared himself for this moment. He knew there was some deep dark secret that would be revealed, but expecting it and hearing it out loud were two very different things.

"We adopted you when you were two days old," his mother said just above a whisper, her eyes pleading with him. "You have to know that we have loved you like our—"

"Just stop!" Ben yelled, no longer able to restrain the anger that had been brewing. He lunged out of his chair wanting to punch something. *Anything.*

"Loved me? Seriously? My ass was *adopted*, and you're just now telling me this shit fifty-some—"

"Boy, watch your mouth!" his father roared and stood to his full height. "Be mad all you want, but what you're not gon' do is curse and yell at your mother." He lifted a hand when Ben started to speak. "Say she's not your mother, and I will knock your ass into next week!"

Chest heaving and his fist balled at his sides, Ben glared at the man he had always looked up to. "I *wasn't* going to say that. I would *never* say that!" he snapped. "But forgive me if I'm a little shocked. It's not every day you find out that the people you have loved and *trusted* the most have been lying to you your whole life."

Huffing and struggling to catch his breath, Ben moved around the room, rubbing his chest. Tears blurred his vision. He couldn't remember the last time he cried, but the ache in his heart was almost unbearable.

"My entire life has been a damn lie," he mumbled. "Then again, I guess you guys didn't lie about everything, especially when you told me that maybe one of my great-great-great grandparents had my eye color. Why didn't you just tell me about the adoption then?"

"You were too young," his mother said weakly.

"What else have you lied about?"

"Come and sit down," Pops demanded as he settled back on the sofa. "We'll tell you anything you want to know."

Ben's blurry gaze drifted to where his mother sat in the center of the sofa. She was one of the sweetest and vibrant women he knew. Seeing her sitting there with her shoulders sagged and her head down gutted him inside.

Reluctantly, he returned to the seat that he had vacated, the one that faced the sofa. It didn't matter how old he was, when Pops gave an order, you obeyed.

Leaning forward, his elbows on his thighs, Ben lowered his head and swiped at his eyes. The tightness in his chest was almost suffocating, but he needed to hear the rest. He needed to know the truth, no matter how painful it would be.

"I want to know everything," he said, unable to stop glaring at the man who had raised him.

Pops cleared his throat, but hesitated before saying, "Your father—"

"He's not my father!" Ben growled before he could stop himself. He might've been pissed at everyone at the moment, but there was one thing he knew for sure. Steven and Katherine Jenkins were his parents. Nothing would ever change that, even though at the moment he was mad as hell.

"Terrance was an only child," Pops continued. "When he was sixteen, his parents were killed in a car accident. He had always been in and out of trouble, nothing too serious, but just…stupid stuff. Anyway, after his parents died, he was lost. He couldn't seem to get his life together, but he always kept in touch with me.

"The summer after he barely graduated from high

school, he started dating this girl and got her pregnant."

Ben's pulse pounded loudly in his ears and his breaths came in short spurts. He struggled to listen as his father told him about people Ben never knew existed. He tried to stay calm and just hear the story about how his biological father had been crazy in love. But all he could think about was how two people who he loved more than life had lied to him his whole life. The people he trusted more than anyone in the world.

"When Terrance found out he was going to be a father, he was thrilled. He had all of these elaborate plans of how he was going to get an apartment, marry this girl, and raise you together."

"The girl had other plans," his mother added. "Terrance might've loved her, but she didn't feel the same about him. She didn't want marriage or…"

"Me," Ben finished bitterly. "What was her name?" he asked even though he already knew the answer.

"Cheryl Foxall. Edward was her father," Pops said. "He was overseas when all of this took place. We don't know how active he was in Cheryl's life. He and Cheryl's mother never married."

Ben rubbed his forehead, willing his headache to ease up. "How did the adoption come about?"

His mother shook her head and dabbed at her eyes with a tissue she plucked from a nearby tissue box. "Terrance begged her not to terminate the pregnancy, telling her that he would do anything she wanted and would take full responsibility for you. He stood by her, but when she was around six months pregnant, Terrance got into some trouble that landed him in jail. It was his third strike."

"Then he got in touch with me and told us about Cheryl and that she was pregnant," Pops added. "We agreed to help any way we could, especially since her mother was dead, and her father was overseas. Everything was fine until a few weeks before she gave birth."

"What happened then?"

"She said that she was putting the baby up for adoption, and there wasn't anything Terrance could do or say to change her mind."

"That's when I told her we would adopt you," his mother said, looking at Ben. His chest tightened at seeing the love glistening in her eyes. "She agreed to let us have you as long as we agreed to a closed adoption. Which was what I preferred."

Ben didn't know what to say. He should probably thank them for their sacrifice, but the anger from earlier was still stirring within him. It was best he didn't say anything for fear of saying something he wouldn't be able to take back.

"Even though Terrance agreed to sign over his rights, he still wanted to be a part of your life in some way."

"I didn't want him anywhere near you," Ben's mother said, her words clipped as she stared down at the crumpled tissue in her hand. "I wanted to keep you far away from both of them. They didn't deserve you."

Pops rubbed her thigh and gave it a little squeeze before she covered his hand with hers.

Growing up, Ben loved the relationship his parents had with each other. They rarely argued and could always be caught kissing, hugging, and holding hands. To this day, they still behaved the same even when they didn't always agree on something.

Pops tossed back the rest of his drink. "When you were a month old, we took you to see Terrance in prison. He couldn't stop thanking us for bringing you, but before we left, he asked us not to bring you back. Even though you were a baby, he didn't want you to see him locked up. He had wanted to wait until he was out of there and doing something with his life."

"You've been talking about him in past tense. What happened to him?" Ben asked, his body wound tighter than a steel spring. Overwhelmed with all that he'd learned, he wasn't sure how much more he could listen to.

"A fight broke out in the prison yard. Terrance hadn't

been in the fight, but got shanked during the brawl. He died in prison."

"*Christ.*" Ben stood and rubbed the back of his neck, trying to ease some of the tension. He knew talking to his parents would reveal things he didn't want to hear, but this was almost too much.

"He was a good guy, Ben. He just made one too many poor choices and was often in the wrong place at the wrong time."

Ben leaned against a nearby wall and rubbed his eyes. He still had questions, but there was one thing that bugged the hell out of him.

"Even if Cheryl wanted nothing to do with me, how could you keep something like this from me?"

His mother stood and moved toward him. Ben wasn't sure what she saw on his face, but she stopped abruptly. "Our plan was to tell you when you were eight. I'm not sure why we chose that number, but we figured you'd be at the age where you could understand. But each year, we put it off, until it never seemed to be the right time.

"Ben, you have to know that we've loved you from the day we brought you home from the hospital. You were *our* son. It didn't matter how you came into this world—"

"But it matters to me!" Ben snapped, then huffed out a breath. His heart ached. It was beating so hard if felt like it would beat right out of his chest. "I'm sorry. I love you guys," he choked out, "But you should've told me. I had a right to know about my birth parents. Instead, I had to find out when I'm in my fifties and after all of them were dead. That's unforgivable."

Turning that thought over in his mind, his anger intensified. How could they have looked at him every day and not think enough to tell him the truth? If for nothing else, they should've told him in order to protect him in other ways. All the girls he had dated in school—heck, for all he knew, he could've been dating his sibling or his cousin.

"I gotta get out of here," he mumbled more to himself

than to them.

"Ben, I know you're angry, but please know that we didn't mean to hurt you," his mother said, swiping at tears. "We love you, honey." She laid her hand on his back and he flinched.

He lifted his hands out in front of him. "I know. I know. I just..." He didn't know what else to say. He needed time. He needed space. More than anything, he needed air.

He yanked the door open and rushed out of the office. He spotted Thomas standing in the hallway near the kitchen.

Immediately Ben wondered if his brother had known. Had all of them known and just not told him?

Thomas glanced down the hall toward the office, and then back at Ben with his brows furrowed. "What's going on?"

"Nothing," Ben said and kept walking. He picked up his pace, practically running to the back door. He needed air.

"Ben!" his brother yelled after him.

"Let him go," their father said.

Yeah, he was going, and he wasn't sure when or if he'd ever be back.

Chapter Twelve

Loud cheers went up in the arena where Makena was watching Ava play basketball. When she found out that the University of Cincinnati's women's team had an away game in Columbus, she and Halle decided to drive up and cheer the team on.

Little did Makena know that they'd start well over an hour late because of technical problems with the game and shot clocks. It was almost ten o'clock at night, and they were just starting the fourth quarter.

It wouldn't have been that big of a deal if she wasn't worried about Ben. When she arrived in Columbus, she received a text from him saying that he was going to see his parents. She didn't want to think that he had intentionally waited until she was out of town to talk to them. But, of course, that was her first thought.

Ben had been distant for the last couple of days, refusing to see her, barely talking to her, and basically shutting her out. He claimed he wasn't mad at her interference. Yet, the tension between them said otherwise. Makena tried giving him space, understanding that he needed it, especially until he talked with his parents.

She just hadn't expected him to shut her out.

"Our girl has the ball," Halle said, her attention locked

on the basketball court where Makena's should've been. Ava wasn't as tall as some of the girls on her team, but her ball-handling skills and hustle down the court made her one of their best players.

Makena shot out of her seat. "Yes! That's my girl!" she screamed when Ava drove to the basket and made it.

"Finally, you're back in the game," Halle said when Makena sat back down. "For a while there, I thought you were going to steal my car and go racing back to Cincinnati to check on your man."

"I still might. It's been a couple of hours, and he's not responding to any of my text messages. I'm starting to worry."

"Yeah, I can understand that, but maybe Ben jumped to conclusions. He's gotten himself all worked up before getting any answers. Edward could be a distant, long-lost relative that no one knows about."

"If you had seen Edward that day he came to the office, you would've saw what I saw. It was like looking at father and son. I'd bet my law degree that Edward is not a distant relative. Ben saw the resemblance, too, and that's what shook him up."

Halle nodded. "Well, I'll think good thoughts for him. I've practiced family law long enough to see a ton of cases like this. Money situations, but mostly secrets, come out after someone dies and families often get ripped apart. I hope that won't be the case this time."

That was part of what had Makena worried. The Jenkins were a tight-knit family, willing to go to battle and support each other under any circumstances. The last thing she wanted was for whatever was going on to draw a wedge between them.

She glanced at her phone again, hoping Ben had responded to one of her text messages. He hadn't. Her concern for him increased, fearing that he had received disturbing news.

She'd give him until the end of the game. If she didn't

hear from him by then, she'd call one of his sons. In the meantime, she sent up a quick prayer that he was all right.

A short while later, the University of Cincinnati's women's team won by four points in a nail-biting finish. Makena and Halle congratulated the team, hugged Ava, and was now getting ready to head back to Cincinnati.

The moment they hopped into the car, Halle blasted the heat. "I can't believe you have me out here freezing my butt off. I should be home cuddled up with Pepper," she said of her black Labrador retriever. "And maybe a good book with a glass of wine."

"You can do that any time. How often do you get to hang out with me and a bunch of other screaming parents?" Makena pulled her cell phone from her small over-the-shoulder purse.

"You're right. Besides sitting next to Mr. Too-Much-Cologne and hearing about how worried you are about your man, it was a fun evening."

Makena tried Ben again, and the call went straight to voicemail. She didn't bother leaving a message, she called his son BJ. After several rings, he picked up.

"Hello," he said, sounding as if he had been asleep.

"BJ, this is Mac."

After a slight hesitation and hearing him moving around, he said, "Hey, Mac. What's going on?"

"I'm sorry to call you so late, but I can't reach your dad. Have you talked to him today?"

"Nah, I haven't talked to him in a few days. Why? Did something happen?" He sounded fully awake now, and Makena wasn't sure what to tell him.

"He hasn't been feeling too well, and I'm in Columbus. I'm heading back to town now, but I wanted to make sure he was all right."

Him not feeling well wasn't a complete lie. Ben hadn't been himself in days, and apparently, she wasn't the only one he'd been keeping his distance from.

"I might be overreacting," she said. "But can you try to

find him? He's not answering his phone."

"Yeah, of course. I'll swing by his house in a few minutes, then give you a call back."

Makena released the breath she hadn't realized she was holding. "That would be great. Thank you."

"Feel better now?" Halle asked when Makena ended the call.

"I won't feel better until I see Ben for myself."

*

Ben stared at the television, the remote control in one hand and his second glass of Jack Daniels in the other. There wasn't a light on in the house, and he had hoped that by now that he would've been able to tune out all the thoughts rolling around in his mind.

No such luck.

He slammed back the remaining dark liquid in his glass and poured another.

Sitting back on the sofa, Ben glanced at the material on the coffee table. After leaving his parents' house, he had stopped by the liquor store, then arrived home and immediately did some research on Cheryl Foxall. He didn't find out much except that she was a virtual assistant for many years. He also found a photo of her that he printed out.

Cheryl was the spitting image of her father, and there was no doubt that Ben was her son. He had her eyes and nose. The rest of his features, were all from the Jenkins' side of the family.

"How could they have not told me?" he said. That question plagued him since leaving his parents' home.

He drained his glass, and sat it on the coffee table. Head spinning, Ben grabbed the edge of the sofa to steady himself. It probably hadn't been the best idea to drink that last glass of Jack so fast.

He sat back gingerly, then stretched out on the sofa and sighed.

What a day, he thought.

Heck, it had been a week for the books. In the last few

days Ben had found out his late grandfather could've been his twin, and had left him a couple of acres of prime real estate. But what topped that was learning that his biological father had been killed in prison, and his birth mother hadn't wanted him.

Then there was Steven and Katherine Jenkins, the only parents he'd ever known. The two people he loved more than he could ever express, and the ones he owed his life to.

The parents he once thought could do no wrong had lied to him for over fifty years.

Now that's unforgivable, was Ben's last thought before drifting off to sleep.

*

"What's wrong with Papa?"

"I'm not sure, yet."

Floating in and out of consciousness, Ben heard the voices that sounded far off in the distance. He just couldn't seem to open his eyes to see who they belonged to. The hammering inside of his skull wasn't helping matters.

"Dad, wake up." Someone shook him, and the banging in Ben's head intensified. "Come on, Dad, wake up."

Ben jerked awake and squinted at the tall figure looming over him. "BJ?" he rasped, barely recognizing his own voice as he struggled to wake up. "What are you doing here?" Ben was surprised he hadn't heard the house alarm, assuming he'd remembered to set it.

"Hey, Papa. Are you alive?" his five-year-old grandson Jayden asked, leaning on Ben's chest and looking at him seriously.

Ben chuckled. "Yeah, I think so. What are you guys doing here?" He sat up slowly, put his feet on the floor, and grabbed his head.

"Daddy said we're making sure you're still alive." Jayden moved away from him and picked up the TV remote. After pushing a few buttons, he landed on the Disney channel.

"Mac sent us," BJ said, and sat next to Ben. "Care to tell me why she's worried about you? And how is it that I didn't even know you were sick."

Ben frowned. "She told you I was sick?"

"Yeah, so what's wrong? Are you hurt?"

"Daddy, can you stop talking loud? I can't hear the TV."

Jayden turned up the volume and Ben smiled. The kid was the best cure for the blues. Ben wished he would've gone to see him earlier in the week. Then maybe he wouldn't have gotten so sucked into the drama that was now his life.

"Jay, why don't you watch TV in your room. I need to talk to your dad a minute," Ben said.

"Okay." Jayden took off in a sprint out of the room.

After BJ was awarded full custody of Jayden a few years ago, Ben had converted BJ's old bedroom into a little boy's paradise. So whenever he visited, he'd feel at home. From a loft bed with a fort beneath it, to a computer and game station, the bedroom had it all.

"Here," BJ handed Ben a glass of water and a bottle of ibuprofen. "If you don't need those yet, based on that half-empty bottle of Jack, you will eventually."

"Thanks," Ben mumbled and immediately took the pills and chased them down with water.

BJ turned the TV volume down. "Care to tell me what has you drinking in the middle of the night in complete darkness?"

"Where to start," Ben said dryly before telling his son about the last few days.

Sharing his story out loud only made Ben feel worse. It was weird to learn, so late in life, that he'd been adopted and might have a whole other family out there somewhere. There was still so much he didn't know about his birth mother's side of the family. He also found it hard to comprehend that this had been able to stay a secret for so long. That was unheard of in the Jenkins family.

"That's crazy," BJ said, looking at Ben as if seeing him for the first time. "How is it possible that you're just finding all of this out? I can't believe Gram and Pops never said anything. More than that, motor-mouth Martina, who sees all and knows all in this family, hasn't said a word. Meaning, I finally know something she doesn't know."

Ben couldn't help but laugh at that. His niece, Martina Jenkins-Kendricks—also known as MJ—was the family's busybody. He loved her to death, but she started more drama in the family than anyone else. BJ was right. If she hasn't mentioned this family secret, maybe it was indeed a secret from everyone. But Ben still found that hard to believe.

"So how do you feel about all of this?" BJ asked.

"I'm mad as hell. Think about it. How would you feel if you found out that everything you thought you knew about yourself, your mother and me, was a lie?"

They both fell silent before BJ said, "Yeah, I guess that would be a little weird. You don't have any deep dark secrets about me that I should know about, do you?"

"Nothing I can think of at the moment, but give me about thirty years. Something might come to mind," Ben said dryly and yawned.

"Well, at least you're sober enough to joke. Are you planning to keep this revelation silent, you know, about you being adopted and all?"

"At this point, I don't care who knows. I hate secrets. Always have, always will. Someone always gets hurt by them, whether they're revealed or not." Ben stood slowly, still feeling a little unbalanced. So much for drinking his problems away. "You and Jay are welcome to stay, but I'm going to bed. Lock up, either way."

"What about Mac? She sounded pretty worried about you. Are you going to call her?"

Ben wasn't ready to talk to Makena. He wanted to believe that he wasn't petty enough to be mad at her for bringing his family secret to light. Yet, if he was honest with himself, deep down, he was a little ticked. She was being her thorough, curious self, but it had been at his expense.

Then again, being adopted had been something he needed to know and had a right to know. Whether he liked the truth or not, it was good he knew part of his history. But right now, he didn't feel like repeating what he'd learned. He just wanted to crawl into bed and pretend that nothing had changed in his life.

"I'll call her later."

Chapter Thirteen

Makena stood at the door of Ben's bedroom to check on him. He was laying on his stomach with his face buried in a pillow, and his arms stretched wide. The striped comforter covered him from the waist down.

The way he was laid out reminded her of Christ hanging on the cross, except she had a view of Ben's muscular arms and his back. His smooth, strong, well-defined back.

Makena shook her head. "I'm pissed at him. I shouldn't be ogling his body," she mumbled as she headed back to the kitchen.

She released a noisy yawn as she started the coffee. Tired and grumpy wasn't a good combination. She had only slept a couple of hours after tossing and turning in the guest room. She probably would've climbed into bed with Ben had they been in the house alone. As it was, BJ and Jayden had stayed the night and left an hour ago.

Leaning a hip against the counter, Makena watched as the coffee brewed. Considering how much BJ said Ben had drank the night before, he'd probably need a strong cup of joe. If she wasn't pissed, she'd make him breakfast. But if he wanted the most important meal of the day, he'd have to make it himself.

On her way back to Cincinnati, BJ had called her as

promised. He told her Ben was all right. He'd had too much to drink and was a little down, but other than that he was fine.

That hadn't been good enough for Makena. When she arrived home, she packed an overnight bag and headed to Ben's house. She needed to see with her own eyes that he was okay. Maybe if he had returned one of her texts, she wouldn't have made the drive.

That was only part of why she was upset with him. He knew she was concerned about the meeting with his parents. Yet, he didn't think enough of her to at least tell her that he was okay, but didn't feel up to talking. Makena could've understood that. If not for BJ, she still wouldn't know anything.

Once the coffee was finished, Makena filled two large mugs and padded back to Ben's room. She set one cup on his night stand, then went to the other side of the bed. Placing her mug down for a minute, she climbed onto the huge bed and then picked it back up.

Bringing the coffee to her lips, she inhaled deeply, appreciating the strong aroma before taking a tentative sip. She sat there drinking the hot brew while listening to Ben snore. The sound wasn't loud and obnoxious, but loud enough to know that he was deep in sleep.

She didn't plan on staying at his house long, but they needed to talk. They never had a problem communicating, and Makena didn't want them to start now. But if he kept pushing her away, they were definitely going to have trouble.

Makena drank more of the coffee before setting the mug on the night stand. She laid her head back against the headboard and closed her eyes. The past couple of weeks had been exhausting. Not only had her and Ben taken their relationship to the next level, but she learned something about herself. She never knew she could be so pushy until she insisted Ben learn more about Edward. Now she prayed that he could find a way to forgive his parents.

"Good morning."

Makena's eyes snapped open, and Ben was sitting up in bed with the coffee mug in his hand.

Had she dozed off?

"Hey," she finally said. "I didn't know you were awake."

"Yeah, because you were asleep." He drank more of the coffee. When she brought it into the bedroom, steam billowed above the rim. Yet, he was practically gulping it. Apparently, she had dozed off.

"How long have you been here?" he asked.

That reminded Makena that she was ticked at him. "I came last night…when you refused to respond to any of my messages."

He sighed and set the mug back on the night stand. Then turned to her. "Sweetheart—"

"Save it. I get that what you learned last night was a shock. I even understand you being upset. What I won't accept is some lame excuse why you couldn't just shoot me a quick text."

He folded his powerful arms, bringing Makena's attention to his bare chest. His body was such a distraction, she was going to need him to put a shirt on so that she could concentrate.

"Like what? What could I have said in a text that would've been enough for you?'

Irritation swirled inside of her. "Why are you acting like a jerk? You could have at least acknowledged that you received my messages. You could've just said, I'm okay. I'll talk to you tomorrow. Heck, you could've even sent a thumbs-up emoji," she snapped, getting madder by the minute. "How would you feel if I treated you like that?"

He held his hands out in front of him as if surrendering. "Okay. Okay. I'm sorry. You're right."

He reached for her hand, and Makena was tempted to snatch it back but she didn't. There was no sense in both of them acting childish.

He kissed the back of her fingers. "I didn't mean to make you worry. I just wasn't in a good place to talk to you last night…or to send emojis."

"I get that, Ben, but if we're going to make this relationship work, you can't be pulling away from me."

"What, like you did to me after Edward died?"

She wanted to tell him that was different, but she couldn't. He was right.

"I'm sorry about that. I didn't handle the situation well. Meeting Edward and seeing how much he resembled you took me by surprise. I battled with myself for weeks on whether to even mention him to you for fear of crossing some ethical line."

"Listen, I get it. I'm not sure how I would've acted under those circumstances, either. And I promise never to pull away from you again. Now, kiss me good morning."

Makena leaned away from him. "Not until you brush your teeth and put some clothes on. Also, we're not done talking. I want us to discuss what happened at your parents' house."

Ben shook his head. "I'd rather we not, but I'm sure you're not going to let it go." Grumbling, he climbed out of the bed, wearing only a pair of striped boxers as he trudged to the bathroom.

Makena got up and refilled their coffee. She returned and set the mugs down just as Ben stepped out of the bathroom, showered and shaved. He had changed into a black T-shirt that hugged his upper body and a pair of black lounging pants.

"Now, can I get some love?" he asked, pulling her into his arms.

He didn't give her a chance to respond. Instead, he covered her mouth with his and kissed her as if he hadn't seen her in weeks. It was impossible to stay mad at him when he reminded her of what she'd been missing the last few days.

"I promise not to disappear on you again," he said as he held her close. "I never want to do anything that will hurt you in anyway. You're too important to me."

Makena's heart softened, and she cupped his cheek. "I

feel the same about you. Now, how about something to eat?"

After filling up on a breakfast of grits, bacon, and eggs, they climbed back into bed. Makena slipped her arm through Ben's and laid her head on his shoulder. The television, hanging on the wall across the room, was on, but the volume was down low.

She loved being with him. Sure, they'd had their share of disagreements over the years, but nothing they weren't able to resolve quickly. She understood how this new development in his life had shaken him. Yet, the unconditional love and respect they had for each other was stronger than ever. Makena would do anything for him just like she knew he would do for her. They would get through this together.

"Have you ever thought about getting married again?" Ben asked.

Makena lifted her head, surprised by the question. "No. After my divorce, I never imagined I'd meet someone that I'd want to marry. What about you? Have you ever thought about it?"

He brushed his lips across hers. "Not until you returned to Cincinnati. Now, I can't imagine *not* getting married."

All Makena could do was stare at him. What could she say to that? Did she love him? Yes. Could she see spending the rest of her life with him? Heck yeah. But marriage? They had just gone from friends to lovers. Wasn't it too soon to even be thinking about marriage?

Instead of asking him that, she asked, "Are you trying to distract me so that I'll stop bringing up the conversation you had with your parents?"

A slow grin spread across his sexy lips. "I wasn't, but if it's working—"

"It's not."

"In that case, let's discuss marriage."

"Ben, would you be serious."

"Sweetheart, I'm dead serious. I love you. You love me. And I'm planning on marrying you one day."

Makena searched his eyes, trying to determine if he was

really serious. "Where is this coming from? We just started dating."

"But I didn't just start loving you," Ben countered.

"With all that's going on in your life, Ben, the last thing you should be thinking about is marriage."

He nodded, looking deep in thought as he studied her. "I might be struggling to forgive my parents, but one thing I've learned from them is to follow my heart. They've been together for over sixty years, and it started with my father telling my mother that he was going to marry her. Mind you, she was still in high school.

"So I don't think me professing my love to you and sharing my intentions is crazy at all. Driving home from my parents' house last night, and replaying in my mind all that they told me, I realized life can change in a heartbeat.

"Take Edward for example. A couple of weeks ago, he was sitting in your office discussing his will. Now he's dead. Our lives can change just like that." He snapped his fingers. "Knowing that, I'm planning to live the rest of my days to the fullest...with you. I love you, sweetheart. We might not get married anytime soon, but just know that marrying you is my ultimate goal."

Ben lowered his head and covered her mouth with his, sending shock waves shooting through her veins. Makena quivered at the tenderness of the passionate kiss. With his profession of love, she didn't think she could love him any more than she did at that moment.

And now was as good a time as any to show him just how much she adored him.

Chapter Fourteen

A couple of hours later, Ben was laying on his back contently with Makena snuggled against his side. He slowly brushed his hand up and down her back, caressing her soft skin. He would never get enough of her. They'd spent much of the day in bed, and he couldn't think of a better way to spend a day off.

She'd been quiet for the last few minutes, and he could almost hear the wheels turning in her mind.

"What are you thinking?" he asked. The way she was tracing his tattoo with her finger was almost soothing enough to lull him back to sleep,

"I'm thinking about you, and what we talked about earlier."

He turned slightly until he was on his side and they were facing each other. "We've covered a lot of topics today. Which one are you referring to?"

"I know you're upset about learning that you were adopted, but—"

"Sweetheart, being adopted is not the issue. The fact that my parents never told me is what bothers me the most. I had no idea. I had a whole other family out there. Whether or not they wanted me is beside the point. My issue is with the two people I have loved all my life and the way they lied to me."

After a slight hesitation, she said, "Yeah, that kinda sucks, but they're your parents. You can't just write them off."

Ben already knew he couldn't just cut them out of his life. They were too much a part of him. But still...

"I've always looked up to my dad," he said. "The older I got, the more I appreciated his integrity and his strength. He's always seemed larger than life, and I've wanted to be like him for as long as I can remember. Then to suddenly find out he's been keeping this type of secret..."

"Honey, he's human," Makena said, cupping his cheek and running the pad of her thumb across his bottom lip. "I bet you can count on one hand how many times he's let you down. Please don't throw away the relationship you have with your parents because of one mistake."

Ben huffed out a breath and rolled onto his back. He stared up at the tray ceiling. He didn't know what his next steps would be.

"After years of loving you as their own," Makena continued, "Your adoption probably wasn't something they thought about that often. You are their son in every way. That's how they saw you back then, and that's how they see you now. Yes, they made a mistake in not being straight with you early on, but, babe, we all make mistakes."

Ben's gut tightened as disappointment filled him, and the inner torment from the night returned. Yeah, everyone made mistakes, but he practically worshiped his parents, especially his father.

"Pops was my hero," he said. "He used to be everything I ever—"

"He's still the man you thought he was before learning about this. And anyone who knows Katherine knows there's nothing in this world she wouldn't do for you or anyone else in the family.

"Baby, you have to figure out how to forgive your mother and father and move on. Remember what you said. Life is short. You can't keep—"

"Mac, you're trying to simplify a difficult situation. I agree with everything you've said, but forgiving them is just not that easy. I don't know how I'm ever going to be able to face them after last night, let alone return to the house."

"Well, you can start by attending Sunday brunch. I have a feeling everyone's going to be there."

Ben shook his head and covered his face with his forearm. "Yeah, all the more reason for me to stay away."

*

"Ben seemed all right when he walked in, but how's he really doing?" Carolyn asked as she dug into her food.

Makena was sitting next to her at the far end of the dining room table, thinking that Ben might've been right about attending the brunch. It might've been too soon. Everyone at the house was afraid to say anything around him for fear of saying the wrong thing. Yet, they kept asking her questions.

"He's handling the news as well as expected. I'm sure, in time, the shock will start to taper off." At least Makena hoped.

Family was everything to Ben. If the tension in the house didn't lighten up, he probably would want to leave early. She'd been thrilled when he told her he was heading downstairs to the theater room to watch the basketball game with the guys. The men in the family usually hung out in the basement either watching sports, playing cards or dominoes, or to just talk trash. She was glad he was making an effort to spend time with them.

"Did you know about Ben's parentage?" Makena asked Carolyn quietly enough that those at the other end of the table couldn't hear.

"I had no clue. Keep in mind, we all were only one or two years apart. So when my parents brought Ben home from the hospital, Sarah, who's the oldest, was probably only eight. Even when we were growing up, I never heard he was adopted."

Makena hadn't known until a few minutes ago that

Carolyn and a few others had been at the house when Ben found out about his birth parents. She didn't know if he had intentionally left that out of his recap to her, or if he had just forgotten to mention it.

"So you and Ben finally decided to stop pretending you weren't dating, huh? I saw the way he kissed you before going downstairs," Carolyn said slyly before grinning. "Details, sister. I want details."

Makena laughed and stood. "I never kiss and tell. I'm going to get some dessert. Do you want anything?"

"Nah, I'm good. Thanks."

When Makena walked into the kitchen, there was still a ton of food left. Like usual, Katherine and the women in the family had outdone themselves. There was everything from pancakes and waffles to smothered fried chicken and rice, Ben's favorite.

She had noticed that Katherine made a few of Ben's favorite dishes even though she hadn't been sure he'd show up. Catfish, collard greens, candied yams, and Katherine's homemade biscuits which she didn't make often, were a few of the items.

"Hey, Mac," Christina said from the kitchen table. "Gram told me to let you know that there's banana pudding in the refrigerator with your name on it."

"Oh good. I was hoping there'd be some this week."

Makena opened the refrigerator. She smiled when she saw the glass bowl covered with a lid and a sticky note with *Makena* scribbled on it.

"Looks like there's enough for all of us." She carried the dish across the room. Besides Christina, another one of Ben's nieces, Jada, was eating at the table, along with Liberty.

"I'm stuffed, but I want to taste it. Let me grab some dessert plates," Jada said. She went to the pantry and returned with paper plates.

A former sheet-metal worker, Jada was also the fashionista of the family. As usual, she looked as if she was about to walk the runway. Wearing a chic asymmetrical jacket, skinny blue jeans, and high-heeled black thigh-high boots, she almost looked out of place in the kitchen.

Instead of returning to the dining room, Makena joined the girls at the kitchen table. The first spoon full of banana pudding to touch her tongue had her moaning with pleasure.

"God, this is good. Even when I follow your grandmother's recipe, mine doesn't taste like this," Makena admitted.

"Nobody makes desserts like Gram," Christina said, but pushed the bowl away, looking like she was about to throw up.

"Why's it so damn quiet around here? Did someone die and not tell me?" Martina, also known as MJ, asked when she burst into the kitchen and made a beeline for the food sitting on the huge center island.

She was usually the first person to arrive, and Makena had wondered where she was.

"So, what's up. The tension in this house is thicker than San Francisco fog. What'd I miss?" She didn't pose the question to anyone in particular, and no one spoke right away. "And where is Gram? I've been here for fifteen minutes, and she hasn't threatened to wash my mouth out with soap for cursing."

"She's in her bedroom," Liberty said. "She's not feeling well."

MJ stopped and looked at each of them at the table. "Gram is never sick. Did something happen?"

Christina, wearing a long, colorful prairie dress that matched her artsy personality, glided over and stood next to MJ. "Did you know Uncle Ben was adopted?"

MJ froze. Her hand hovered over the dinner rolls before she looked up. Eyes narrowed and lips pursed, her gaze bounced around to everyone in the kitchen. Yet, she said nothing, which was very telling.

"Oh. My. God. You knew," Christina shrieked. "Your butt can't keep nothin', especially a secret. How is it that you knew and we didn't know?"

Makena wondered the same thing. MJ was that family member who drove everyone nuts. Butting into people's business, picking on everyone about one thing or another, she was the one who usually started trouble.

"Start talking," Liberty said, approaching MJ on the other side.

"Never mind how I knew. I just know things," she finally said. "How'd you guys find out?" Then she looked at Makena, and her eyes grew wide. "Oh, wow. Uncle Ben knows?"

Makena nodded.

Christina folded her arms across her chest. "MJ, where have you been all week? We found out a few days ago. I was expecting you to come in here blabbing about it in that uncouth way you usually do."

MJ ignored the barb and continued piling food on her plate. "Me and Paul snuck away for a few days. Damn, though. This is why I hate leaving town. The moment I do, all the juicy stuff happens. So what'd I miss?" She set the plate down on the table and dropped into the chair next to Jada.

Makena's attention went to the mound of food on MJ's plate. She had never in her life seen a woman who could put away so much food and probably only wore a size four. Yet, her and her mother, Carolyn, didn't seem to gain an ounce of weight despite how much they ate.

Christina and Jada filled MJ in on what took place during the past week. Makena hated hearing them discuss Ben, but that's how the family was. They didn't think anything about being in each other's business.

"He had to be pissed." MJ shook her head, a look of concern on her face. "I'm surprised he came to brunch. Was that your idea, Mac?"

"Yeah," she said, pushing the banana pudding around on the plate. "I had hoped that with being around family, he'd remember how much he's loved."

"Grampa and Gram were wrong in not telling him

115

sooner," Jada said, shaking her head. "If it was me, I'd be pissed."

"Oh, please. You probably were adopted too," MJ said between bites. "'Cause ain't nobody around here as bougie as you."

"The important thing *is*," Liberty interrupted, "that Uncle Ben knows now. We have to make sure he also knows that nothing has changed. We love him all the same."

MJ grunted. "Of course, nothing has changed. He's still my favorite uncle."

Christina chuckled. "Don't let my dad hear you say that. He thinks he's the coolest and the favorite," she said of Thomas.

"Oh, CJ, speaking of secrets," MJ pointed her fork at her, "Is it true that you're prego? I guess you and the thug lawyer screwing in Gram's downstairs bathroom finally paid off, huh?"

Christina's mouth dropped open and then she glared at MJ. "Ugh, I can't *stand* you! Why can't you just be a normal human being like every—"

"Wait. What?"

"You're pregnant?"

Liberty and Jada spoke at once and then shrieked. They were out of their seats so fast, one of the chairs toppled over when they lunged for Christina. Excitement filled the space that was somber a moment ago as they all talked at the same time.

All the while, MJ kept eating, not caring that she had delivered news that CJ probably wasn't ready to share.

Taking it all in, Makena shook her head and laughed.

Family. Gotta love 'em.

Chapter Fifteen

"There you are," Ben said, catching Makena coming out of the family room. "Come with me."

She slipped her hand into his. "Are we leaving?"

"Soon, but my parents want to talk to me first."

Makena pulled up short in the middle of the hallway. "They probably want to talk to you privately. You go ahead. I'll meet you in—"

"No, I want you with me. Anything they say to me, you can hear it, too."

They walked down the long hallway hand in hand and flashbacks from the other night filled Ben's mind. He'd been a wreck coming and going that evening. His emotions had been all over the place. This time though, he was prepared for anything his parents had to say. Besides, having Makena by his side made him feel like he could handle anything.

As they approached the office door, Ben thought about what he wanted to say to his parents. He hadn't seen much of either of them while at the brunch, which was unusual. Knowing them, they had stayed out of sight for his benefit, not wanting him to feel uncomfortable. That was the type of people they were. Their kids' happiness always came first.

Ben had planned to talk to them before leaving anyway. He owed them both an apology. This was as good a time as any to give it.

The office door was open, but he knocked before entering.

"Hey you two. I'm glad you're here," Pops said. He was standing behind his desk with an envelope in his hand.

Ben's mother stood from the sofa and walked toward them. "Makena, I'm glad you're here too," she said as she embraced them both.

Guilt pierced Ben's chest when his mother wrapped her arms around him. He held on to her a little longer, hoping she could feel how much he loved her. They had always had a special bond, and he hated the way he'd left things the other day.

"I owe you guys an apology," he said, releasing his mother and reaching for Makena's hand. Touching her gave him strength that he didn't realize he needed. "The way I stormed out of here the other night was disrespectful, and I'm sorry. I love you guys, and—"

"And you don't owe us an apology," his mother interrupted. "You had every right to be angry. But I hope you know how special you are to us. We love you so much and have always thought of you as a gift from God. I...*we*," she glanced at Pops, "realize that we handled this situation all wrong. But please know that we have always, always had your best interest in mind."

Ben straightened when his father rounded the desk. It was an involuntary move, but Pop's powerful presence had that effect on him. His father made him want to stand as tall and proud as he did.

Pop pointed to the sofa. "Go ahead and have a seat."

Ben and Makena sat next to each other on the sofa while his parents sat in the tall-back Queen Anne chairs that faced the sofa.

"We should've told you everything the moment you were old enough to understand. That's my fault," Pops said quietly, looking more uncomfortable than usual. "Just like with your brothers and sisters, your safety and well-being has always been our top priority. Your mother and I made decisions regarding you kids based on what we thought was best. We were wrong in this case."

Ben felt their anguish with each word. He didn't want them to feel guilty, he just wanted to understand their decision.

"Did you ever consider that I might find out from someone else?" Ben asked.

His mother nodded. "Yes, when you were younger I did, but it never seemed to be the right time to tell you. After a while, the years kind of got away from us." She gave a little laugh, and Ben smiled.

She often said the older you get, the faster time goes. He could relate, because lately his days seemed to fly by.

"Like we told you the other day," his mother continued, "we planned to tell you before you went to middle school. Then more years went by, and we just never said anything. When we heard that Cheryl died, we thought that might be a good time to tell you, but... Honestly, son, there never seemed to be a right time, especially as you got older."

"Personally, I didn't want you to know about Terrance or Cheryl," Pops said. "You were *my* son and that's how I always saw you."

"Yeah, we both felt that way," his mother added. "I thought Cheryl would try and get you back. She actually told me that she might change her mind. The moment we signed the papers, I told her that if she ever came near you, she would regret ever meeting me."

"I think your exact words were '*if you ever come near my son, I will rip your hair out from the roots.*'" Pops laughed and the rest of them joined in.

Ben could totally see his mom saying something like that. She was the sweetest person he knew, but fiercely protective of her family. People often mistook her kindness for weakness until they stepped out of line. Then she was quick to let them know who they were dealing with.

"We never heard from Cheryl again, but Steven kept

track of her and knew of her father. We don't know when Edward learned about you, though. He and Cheryl were estranged from each other when you were born."

The room fell silent, and the full weight of what his parents went through for him settled around Ben.

"I'm grateful for you guys," he said, emotion clogging his throat. "Thank you for saving my life and for loving me unconditionally. You gave me the type of childhood that some kids can only dream of, and you have always supported me. I owe you everything."

When he stood, so did everyone else in the room. His father pulled him into a hug and held him so tight, Ben was sure he'd end up with a couple of bruised ribs, but it would be worth it.

"You don't owe us anything," his father said before releasing him.

Then Ben hugged his mother, the first love of his life...the woman who had always been an example of kindness and grace. How could he have doubted their intentions? For over fifty years, they'd treated him like a special gift and loved him unconditionally. For that, he would be forever grateful.

"I received a letter yesterday," Pops said. He went back to the desk and lifted the envelope he'd been holding when Ben walked in. "It's from Edward. Based on what he says, it appears he wrote it after he met Makena. According to the mailman, it got lost because of the illegible handwriting. Our address was misread, or something like that. Anyway, the letter turned up and the mailman delivered it yesterday."

"Interesting timing," Ben said when Pops handed it over. He pulled it from the envelope and skimmed it.

"Read it out loud," Pops instructed. "Edward mentions Makena in the letter."

Makena's brows rose and they all retook their seats.

To: Steven Jenkins,
You don't know me, but I know of you and your family. I'm Ben's

grandfather. His mother didn't tell me about him until she was on her deathbed. I know legally I'm not to have any contact with him, but I couldn't leave this earth without saying my peace. He's grown up to be a fine young man. He's a good-looking kid, if I say so myself.

Ben chuckled.

I've watched Ben's life unfold from afar. You did a good job raising him. When I found out he was dating an estate attorney, Makena, I thought it was a sign from God. I couldn't help but pay her a visit. If you see fit to tell Ben about this letter, tell him I said he has good taste. She's beautiful. If only I was thirty years younger...

Ben smiled and looked up at Makena who had tears in her eyes and her hand on her chest. Edward was right, she was beautiful, and Ben was grateful that she was his. He only wished that he'd had the pleasure of meeting Edward. He now understood why Makena tried to figure out a way for them to meet. She'd said he was charming, and Ben could see that in the letter.

He went back to reading.

I hope I didn't scare Makena too much. She looked at me like she was seeing a ghost. Before going to see her, I was afraid she would tell Ben about me. But deep down, I think I wanted her to tell him. That probably would've caused all type of legal problems, but I wouldn't care. I'll probably be dead soon. I have a lung condition, and I'm as old as dirt.

Again, Ben smiled, but his heart ached for the grandfather he never knew, but would've liked.

Anyway, Makena was very professional and sweet. She probably won't tell him about me before I leave this earth, which is okay. I'm glad I got to meet someone who is special to my grandson. It made me feel a little closer to him.

Steven, I'm writing you because I wanted to thank you for raising him. I doubt I could've done a better job, though I would have loved to have the opportunity. My daughter and I never had a good relationship. By the time Ben was born, we didn't talk at all. I was surprised she even told me about him before she died, but it was probably to torture me. She knew I would honor the agreement she made with you and your wife.

If you see fit, let my grandson know that I'm proud of the man he's become. I left him the land because I wanted to leave a legacy to my only heir. I know he will do something great with the property.

Oh, and tell him to put a ring on that young lady's finger soon. She's a keeper. Tell him to marry her. Life is too short and precious to not spend with someone special. I missed out, and I don't want him to make the same mistake I did.

Thank you again for raising a fine young man.

Sincerely,

Edward Benjamin Foxall

Benjamin?

"Wait. I was named after him?" Ben looked at his parents in shock. He hadn't noticed Edward's middle name on any of the documents that Mike had sent over.

"Cheryl gave you the name, and I thought it was a nice, strong name," his mother said and shrugged. "I didn't realize it was her father's name."

For a minute, Ben sat stunned. It was going to take him a while to process the past couple of weeks, but the letter gave him some clarity and closure that he needed.

"Pops, thanks for letting me read this. It means a lot." He handed the letter to him, but his father waved it off.

"Keep it. I didn't know the guy, but I'm glad he reached out in his own way."

"Yeah, me too." Ben stood and reached for Makena. He pulled her into a tight hug and whispered in her ear. "Thank you for always standing by me and loving me enough to make me seek the truth. I love you, sweetheart."

"I love you more." She leaned back and looked at him with tears in her eyes, and then she smiled. "Will you marry me?"

Ben's heart skidded to a halt. When he realized she was serious, he burst out laughing. "I thought you'd never ask."

Epilogue

A month later…

"Are we really going to do this?" Makena asked as she and Ben stood on a busy sidewalk on the strip in Las Vegas.

He smiled down at her, then at the tiny wedding chapel in front of them. He released her hand and slid his arm around her waist.

"I'm game if you still are."

Butterflies fluttered inside Makena's stomach as excitement traveled through her body. Even though she had never planned to marry again, she couldn't wait to become Mrs. Benjamin Jenkins.

She would never forget the day he officially proposed to her. He had driven her out to the land that Edward had left them. Makena thought they were just going to check it out. He told her that he was still trying to decide what to do with the property. Whatever he did, he wanted it to be something that would honor Edward.

While they were there, Ben found an area, in the middle of nothing but trees and dropped down on one knee. He presented her with the most beautiful two-carat French-set halo diamond engagement ring. Of course she said yes. The last couple of months had been an emotional roller coaster for both of them, but they made it. They were really going to do this.

"Papa, can we hurry up?" Jayden said, when he ran up to them.

He'd been standing a few feet away with Ava, BJ, and Ben's oldest son, Antonio, as they discussed their plans for the evening. "Daddy said I can go to the M&M's store when we finish. So can we hurry?"

When Ben mentioned she and him taking a trip, Makena was all in. He could've asked her to go to the moon with him and she would've gone. Then he proposed that they elope, which she thought was a brilliant idea. But when he suggested they invite their kids, she remembered why she loved him so much. Family always came first for him. Including their children and his grandson in this important next step was the best idea ever.

Antonio strolled over and opened the door to the chapel. "Y'all gon' do this or what?"

"Yes!" Jayden said, jumping up and down and ran into the building.

Everyone laughed.

"Somehow, I don't think his excitement has anything to do with you two getting married," BJ said as he followed his son inside. Ava was right behind them.

"You ready?" Ben asked Makena. The love in his beautiful eyes made her heart leap in her chest.

"I'm definitely ready."

She couldn't wait to start their new life together.

*

If you enjoyed this book by Sharon C. Cooper,
consider leaving a review on any online book site, review site or social
media outlet.

Join Sharon's Mailing List

To get sneak peeks of upcoming stories and to hear about giveaways that Sharon is sponsoring, go to https://sharoncooper.net/newsletter to join her mailing list.

ABOUT THE AUTHOR

Award-winning and bestselling author, Sharon C. Cooper, is a romance-a-holic - loving anything that involves romance with a happily-ever-after, whether in books, movies, or real life. Sharon writes contemporary romance, as well as romantic suspense and enjoys rainy days, carpet picnics, and peanut butter and jelly sandwiches. She's been nominated for numerous awards and is the recipient of Emma Awards (RSJ) for Author of the Year 2019, Favorite Hero 2019 (INDEBTED), Romantic Suspense of the Year 2015 (TRUTH OR CONSEQUENCES), Interracial Romance of the Year 2015 (ALL YOU'LL EVER NEED), and BRAB (book club) Award - Breakout Author of the Year 2014. When Sharon isn't writing, she's hanging out with her amazing husband, doing volunteer work or reading a good book (a romance of course). To read more about Sharon and her novels, visit www.sharoncooper.net

Connect with Sharon Online:

Website: https://sharoncooper.net

Join Sharon's mailing list: https://bit.ly/31Xsm36

Facebook fan page: http://www.facebook.com/AuthorSharonCCooper21?ref=hl

Twitter: https://twitter.com/#!/Sharon_Cooper1

Subscribe to her blog: http://sharonccooper.wordpress.com/

Goodreads:
http://www.goodreads.com/author/show/5823574.
Sharon_C_Cooper

Pinterest:
https://www.pinterest.com/sharonccooper/

Instagram:
https://www.instagram.com/authorsharonccooper/

Other Titles

Reunited Series (Romantic Suspense)
Blue Roses (book 1)

Secret Rendezvous (Prequel to Rendezvous with Danger)

Rendezvous with Danger (book 2)

Truth or Consequences (book 3)

Operation Midnight (book 4)

Stand Alones
Something New

("Edgy" Sweet Romance)

Legal Seduction

(Harlequin Kimani – Contemporary Romance)

Sin City Temptation

(Harlequin Kimani – Contemporary Romance)

A Dose of Passion

(Harlequin Kimani – Contemporary Romance)

Model Attraction

(Harlequin Kimani – Contemporary Romance)

Soul's Desire

(Contemporary Romance)

www.ingramcontent.com/pod-product-compliance
Lightning Source LLC
Chambersburg PA
CBHW030234180626
46810CB00008B/3119